CALLING EARTH III

FIGHT FOR HUMANITY'S FUTURE

Shirley Battie

ISBN: 978-1-9995949-1-6

First published in 2020

OTHER BOOKS
BY SHIRLEY BATTIE

Calling Earth   volume one and two

Being Human

Spirit Speaks

Beyond the Stairs

Channelling

LITTLE OWL CARDS
72 inspirational messages

www.littleowlonline.co.uk

DEDICATION

To all those on and off this planet Earth, currently and from the past, who work tirelessly towards a bright future for our children who will inherit what is to come. I dedicate this book to all who endeavour to bring awareness and evidence to the general public that we are not alone and never have been.

ACKNOWLEDGMENT

I thank all those who have read volume one and two of CALLING EARTH, and who have taken the time to comment and write reviews. I thank them also for their patience in waiting for this final volume. They thought it was never coming.

I thank all my friends who have had to put up with my determination to get this trilogy out there. I thank Verna Green and David Green for their invaluable proofreading and encouragement throughout.

HOW IT ALL BEGAN

A small, wiry and rather elderly lady stood before Richard, clutching a bundle of papers pushed roughly into a brown envelope. She calmly placed the package on the desk in front of him. She peered at him over the rim of her glasses, held his gaze and simply said, "You need to read this." As producer of a popular TV programme Richard was not used to being rudely disturbed in this way, and would normally have seen her out, manuscript in hand. On this occasion, for some unfathomable reason, he hesitated. There was a force to her, an intent that was disarming. Still holding her gaze and taking his time he removed the papers from the envelope.

He considered the ominous words heading the final bundle of papers before him.

**THE HUMAN RACE MAY DIVIDE.
YOU ARE ALL ONE WITH YOUR CREATOR, AS ARE ALL SENTIENT BEINGS EVERYWHERE THROUGHOUT THE UNIVERSE. THERE ARE MULTIDIMENSIONAL BEINGS ON MULTIPLE LEVELS. MONITOR YOUR THOUGHTS; EVERYTHING HAPPENING IN YOUR WORLD IS A RESULT OF THOUGHTS. REPLACE FEARFUL THOUGHTS WITH ONES THAT ARE POSITIVE AND LOVING.
EXTREME POSITIVE AND NEGATIVE ENERGIES MAY ALREADY BE TOO FAR APART TO MERGE AND NOT ABLE TO OCCUPY THE SAME SPACE.
THERE MAY BE A DIVISION OF TIMELINES AHEAD FOR THE HUMAN RACE**

Richard took his time. He absentmindedly put the pen he was holding to his head and scratched it. A division of timelines for the Human Race? He read on for a few pages unable to put the manuscript down.

"Leave it with me. I'll give it consideration," he said, not really believing it would go far. But here it is, the powerful tale she brought for him that day.

CONTENTS

CALLING EARTH III

FIGHT FOR HUMANITY'S FUTURE

CHAPTER ONE

WHERE IS SAFETY?

Aye, age old in this warfare,
The eternal struggle between darkness and light
Fiercely is it fought through all the ages
Using strange powers hidden to man.

The Emerald Tablets of Thoth

Gork, the terrible one stomped and roared like a wild beast as he thrashed about the enclosed space of his confinement. His attendants seemed to shrink in size as he passed them. The walls surrounding them all showed terrifying scenes of death and destruction, reflecting the awesomeness of his black soul. A hot blast like a draught from hell followed him as he stormed up and down.

"I *will* not be held in this way. Who do the Galactic Spiritual Council of the Confederation think they are? They do not have jurisdiction over me, The Great Gork."

"Well, you did break the rules by entering The Master's inner sanctum", ventured one brave attendant.

"And," said another, "you also broke the rules of Motherships' neutrality status which is ordained by the Confederation and maintained by the Council".

The enraged roar that came from Gork shook the fabric of the enclosure like a clap of thunder. "I will *not* be contained. They will see what I can do when I return to Earth. I have friends and status there."

"You will have to be released first," said a short spiny beast with a bark like a dog.

"Not a problem," snorted Gork.

His group of attendants shrank back and gathered into a little corner for safety. Maybe they were on the wrong side after all?

***

Another discussion was taking place in the safety of Master M's inner sanctum on the same Mothership. Adam, Kate and her father Jacob grouped together and watched Master M closely, who appeared to be communicating with someone they couldn't see. His golden dome shaped head bowed so low, they wondered if perhaps he had dropped off to sleep.

Adam put his arms around Kate holding her tight, and directed a despairing look at Master M. "What are we going to do? We can't let her go back home and she can't stay here."

Master M appeared not to be listening, his mind was clearly elsewhere.

"Be quiet. Can't you see he is asking the Spiritual Galactic Council," whispered Sechem, the blue time traveller. "They will know what to do."

"It's taking him such a long time. We must do something soon. Kate and Jacob can't stay here too long in their human form density." It was Jamère, the joker who looked worried now. He noticed that Kate had suddenly gone limp like a wilted plant in Adam's arms.

"Shush! Master M is coming back to us." Adam brushed his blond hair away from his eyes, straightened his back and waited.

The Master blinked his large, blue eyes, like camera shutters operating at top speed. He shook his head, as if to clear his senses. "They have decided." He coughed loudly as he looked round the room. "Are you paying attention," he said rather unnecessarily.

Everyone tensed. Was it going to be bad news? Could they handle it? Adam held his breath.

"It has been agreed by all that Kate and her father Jacob must go to America." A gasp of horror came from them all. Jamère and Sechem remained silent

"But that is throwing them to the wolves." Adam's heart began to thump with fear. He tightened his grip on Kate as he noticed she was still hardly breathing. "Kate, wake up," he cried, shaking her hard. But there was no response.

***

Back in the forest clearing near AWE, *(the nuclear centre)* in Aldermaston, from where Kate and her father Jacob had vanished a day ago, a confused group of men were gathered together, grumbling and muttering among themselves. The uniformed men chasing Kate and her father, had eventually found a way round the tree that had inexplicably fallen and blocked their way; but the delay in doing so had caused them to lose their target. Silas Pearce, immaculate as ever, stood motionless in the clearing in the woods, staring into space. Suddenly he ground his fist into his palm. He looked like a man about to explode. Helga, on the other hand, totally exasperated by the search did explode with a huge enraged shout.

"Damn it, they must be somewhere. They can't all have vanished off the face of the Earth."

Her words caused one of the men to titter. She swung round, furious. He stepped back quickly, thinking for one dreadful moment that she would strike him across the face. Then she too stepped back as she realised she mustn't lose her cool. She needed to make a decision, and soon.

"We have to report back," she said curtly. Her lip curled. "Silas? Are you coming or are you going to stand there staring like a shop dummy?"

"Um, er, oh yes," Silas said as he brought his attention back to the situation. "Let's get back to the hotel and collect our things. We can book our flights to DC from there."

Helga snorted. She knew he had no idea how they were going to explain to Gork and those in charge. They would be furious, and it would be she who took the blame, not Silas.

***

Becoming aware Kate opened her eyes very, very slowly. She felt alone and abandoned as she realised she was no longer in the safety of the Mothership. Where was she? It was then that she noticed a dark 'thing' crawling towards her. She tried to focus, to see more clearly, but it was hard to make out what the 'thing' was. A faint smell invaded her nostrils and reminded her of - - - what was it? She had no more time to wonder how she'd got there and why, for the black mass was gathering speed. It was closing in on her feet. She edged backwards. Suddenly, and without any warning, an enormous foot slammed down, forming a barrier between it and her. She looked up. The largest, tallest creature she had ever seen was staring down at her with the deepest of blue eyes. He was dressed in a leather outfit of many colours stitched together. He appeared to be amused and had the faintest expression of a smile.

"Don't worry about it," he said. "but it's not quite harmless." The large person laughed, a huge guffaw. "It shouldn't have got out. We try to keep it, them contained."

Kate scrambled to her feet. "What's that pungent smell?" she asked. "What am I doing here? Where am I and where are my friends?"

"Oh, the smell is always with it, that's how we know it's around. It is very intelligent and has its own mind, believe me. It's just as well it didn't touch you."

"What is it called?" Kate edged back and kept her distance.

"We call it Black Goo for want of a better name." he laughed again, and Kate relaxed just a little. She still didn't know how or why she was there. The tall man seemed kindly, and yes, it was a man, a giant. Did they really exist? She watched as he placed a large transparent container over 'the thing'. At once it became agitated, very cross, and appeared to shake the cage.

Kate stamped her foot. This was getting beyond a joke if this was one of Jamère's doing. "Why am I here and how did I get here?"

The Giant sat on the floor and gestured to her to do the same. "We are on the same level now," he explained. "First of all, let me tell you about this so-called Black Goo, this species, and then you might understand why you are here right now."

Kate sighed. Oh so this was another test, was it?

"No it's not a test," the giant grunted.

Oh dear, yet another who could read her thoughts. Kate settled down to listen. It was clear she was not going anywhere in a hurry.

"You need to be able to recognise the two types of Goo since you are here. To put it very simply, there is the good kind and the awfully bad kind. Their existence started in different ways. One kind, the bad kind arrived on meteorites long before humans existed on Earth. The other which comes from inside the Earth, is still there and will always be there. When your deep-sea divers see plumes of smoke emitted through funnels, they call it Black Smoke. That my dear sweet girl is the good, loving, Black Goo.

The Goo that comes from meteorites is an alien species and has no love, and if you come into contact it will destroy your heart through your subconscious. It is demonic. Its purpose is to destroy love on any planet it reaches."

Kate shook her head in disbelief. "This cannot be. I don't believe it."

The Giant sighed. "You are here to distinguish between the two kinds, for you may meet both on your journeys, or my dear, you may not. But it is well to be prepared. The fluid crystal that is extracted from the alien type stones, doesn't like to be observed and gets angry. It is an artificial intelligence designed to self-replicate and self-learn. You need to be sensitive to your feelings if in proximity to them and steer clear. There are deposits of it around the world, some of which are known by some rulers that I must not name, and used by them. They have property in these places. One is in Paraguay, another in central Germany, another in The Falklands, and in a little island in the South Atlantic called Thule. This is why many people feel that those who rule them may be psychopaths. They have been infected by this virus. The objective of this artificial intelligence is to destroy the planet it is on and move on. Fortunately it is monitored and contained by the Confederation." The Giant helped Kate to her feet and when she lost her balance, he steadied her.

"I am not going to any of those places, so I don't see a problem." Kate dusted herself off and looked around for a way out. The Black Goo under the container appeared to be furious. The urge to kick it and kill it almost overwhelmed her.

"Oh, don't do that," the Giant shouted in alarm. "Can't you see the effect it's demonic nature is already trying to have you affected? Come away."

Kate began to cry. Was it so easy to change one's nature? She definitely wasn't going anywhere near the places he told her of.

"What is the purpose of showing me this? I can't see where I come in." Kate's lip quivered. "Take me back to the Mothership. They'll be worried."

The Giant put a large hand on her shoulder. "Don't take on so. You were lucky I was here when you arrived. I didn't bring you here, I had no intention of showing you the Goo. Your arrival was as much a surprise to me as to you."

"I'm confused." Tears began to roll down her face. It was all too much. Where were the others? Why didn't they come?

***

Back on the Mothership, Adam rubbed Kate's seemingly lifeless hands. "What is happening to her? Master M, please do something." Adam's panic was written all over his face. "Help her." Adam bent over to kiss Kate. "Wake up sweetheart."

Sechem looked up, exasperated. "This is not Sleeping Beauty in a fairy tale, Adam. It is obvious she is right out. She is not here. Something is wrong." He turned to Master M. "Please, do something!"

Jamère moved across to the pair. "Can't you see? Master M is already connecting with the Galactic Confederation Command Council again to find out why she is this way. Be patient," He said it in such a calm voice that Adam relaxed a little and waited.

"This is Gork's doing," Jamère put in unhelpfully.

"Shush. Wait a moment. Can't you see Master M is coming back to us now," Sechem whispered.

The Master was indeed back. He rubbed his large eyes, blinked a few times, folded his arms and smiled so sweetly at them all that they too smiled.

"It was indeed Gork's handiwork. Even though he is confined his mind is not and he was able to detach Kate's etheric body from her physical form."

To their amazement Master M looked as if he was about to laugh and had trouble keeping a straight face.

"But, but, stammered Adam. "Here she is limp and seemingly lifeless. I don't see anything to laugh about."

"Let me explain," Master M said. "But first we need to have her back safe and sound, don't we? She needs an explanation too." They all nodded vigorously.

"Look," Sechem shouted. "She's coming back to us."

Kate twitched a few times, stretched and broke free from Adam's arms, and as she looked around at them all, she said rather crossly,

"Where were you? I needed you."

"We're glad to see you back," they all said in unison. "What happened?"

Kate told them about the Giant and the Goo types. They erupted in questions until Master M held his hand up to silence them.

"Let me tell you and then you will understand. Kate, Gork's mind took you and placed you in danger, hoping and expecting you would be changed to a very different personality. If the Goo had touched you it might have succeeded. You did have an angry moment there, didn't you? Fortunately the Galactic Confederation Command Council were keeping a close watch on him, guessing he would try something. It was they who sent the Giant into that situation, to safeguard you. It also served a purpose, of teaching you more. You were never in real danger and have learned an important lesson."

"I don't like lessons of that kind," Kate snapped back. "Why are you laughing?"

"I am thinking that Gork is getting a lesson he isn't enjoying right now." He's breaking too many rules and may be banished from Galactic Confederation meetings in future. If he is not careful, his powers will be taken from him altogether."

But Adam still looked worried. "We must still decide what to do next." He held Kate's hand more tightly, as if afraid if he let go, she would disappear.

***

Back in DC intense pain shot through the old General's arthritic hand as he thumped the hard desk. He tried not to wince as he raised his arm for permission to speak. His usual stern and not tolerating any nonsense expression changed to one indicating a physical weakness he had no control over. He knew that those who knew him well, respected, and almost venerated him for his past actions in service, but he also suspected that they thought he was now past his best.

He banged the desk again. "What I demand to know is why haven't we heard from Colonel Adam Fenshawe on the matter of Time Travel selections? Why isn't he here at this meeting? I need an answer *now.*"

The chairman of the meeting, a thin foxy looking, sharp eyed man, looked at the General, sitting stiff and erect, with cold and intense dislike. It was time the old guy retired gracefully. He knew the General still expected and hoped his much-loved, ambitious teenage grandson would be chosen for a Jump Room assignment but had not heard anything to that effect.

The crusty old General sensed that even the Chairman wished he too could have that experience for himself although he was aware that training began early with young, fit kids, not mature men like himself, or the chairman.

His thoughts drifted, as it was in the habit of doing recently. His mind remembered the scientists involved discovered that through the consciousness of a human or alien mind, the ship sets a desired destination which opens up a worm hole in front of the ship, which transports you to the desired destination. A receiving end catcher

Jump Room was needed if you wished to go from place to place.

His reliable sources told him that the U.S. government had identified 153 "synthetic quantum environments" (SQEs) constructed by the Greys, because they contained new land that might be territorially acquired. Time travel could make this happen, which is why the U.S. government was actively discovering and exploring these SQEs, with a view to making them part of the United States.

During negotiations, the Greys indicated that the system of "synthetic quantum environments" had been built by them for purposes of conditioning and educating humanity to be able to sustain a future role among organized intelligent civilizations in space and in the inter-dimensional multi-verse. Educating humanity? Now there was a thought. He needed to do more research into this.

Perhaps it was not such a good idea after all for his grandson to be chosen. That worrying thought brought him out of his reverie in time to hear the chairman saying, "Yes, indeed, why isn't Colonel Adam Fenshawe here?" He looked around the assembled gathering, hoping for an answer that would satisfy the old man.

"Well, he is absent rather a lot. Perhaps he has a girlfriend. That would dispel any rumours that he is gay, wouldn't it?" shouted the same red-haired young man who had attended previous meetings and who had accosted Adam with unanswered questions when they were leaving.

The General, recognised for his strict adherence to protocol, also knew that this Chairman did not like and would not allow shouting, whatever the reason.

"Sit down my boy," the Chairman commanded sternly. "We will look into why Colonel Fenshawe is not here when he has been ordered to attend." Secretly he was glad that the Colonel was absent since he had a tendency to raise difficult questions of his own, to which he had no satisfactory answers.

The old General kept disappointment from showing on his face and again asserted his authority. “Let’s get down to our other business,” he said frowning. “What are we going to do about the weather programme? How effective are the chemtrails? Are they having the desired effect?”

The young red-haired man was not going to be quiet, despite the earlier reprimand. “Never mind the weather. It is certainly dumbing down the people, isn’t it? The chemicals are being leeched into animals and vegetation. Of course it is having an effect. Is it the effect you really want?”

Several hands went up requesting permission to speak. The Chairman blanched and pointed at the one person he considered to be least problematic.

“You sir”, he said. “What is it you have to say?”

Congressman Alleyne, an extremely rotund man in a black suit that was clearly too tight and black tie hoisted himself to his feet. He blew out his already full cheeks, causing the chairman to think he was about to spit something out.

“Well, I am beginning to see signs of disorder in my own grandchildren. It is distressing to see at times. They were always so healthy and now they have breathing problems and multiple allergies. Do you think this has anything to do with chemtrails?”

Another civilian allowed to be present because of his scientific knowledge and training raised his hand and was given the nod to speak. As he stood up the various security passes hanging round his neck, jingled together as if saying *pay me attention*. He coughed importantly behind a hand festooned with rings and waited a moment or two for all members to give him full attention. He cleared his throat prior to speaking.

“Gentlemen, may I quote from scientific journals as indicated in the papers before me?” He scanned the gathering to see if all were paying attention. He looked down at his papers and began to read. “Such spraying will saturate the ground, water and vegetation with high levels of aluminum. Normally, aluminum is poorly absorbed from the GI tract, but nanoaluminum is absorbed in much higher amounts. This absorbed aluminum has been shown in a number of organs and tissues, including the brain and spinal cord. Inhaling this environmentally suspended nanoaluminum also produces a tremendous inflammatory reaction within the lungs, which will pose a significant hazard to children and adults with asthma and pulmonary diseases.”

He looked hard and long at the Chairman to see if this had an effect before continuing. The Chairman was yawning. Undeterred the scientist continued reading.

“Are you aware that there are 3 billion fewer birds on the planet than fifty years ago? My major concern is that there is evidence that we are spraying tons of nanosized aluminum compounds. It has been demonstrated in the scientific and medical literature that nanosized particles are infinitely more reactive and induce intense inflammation in a number of tissues. Especially concerning is the effect of these nanoparticles on the brain and spinal cord. A growing list of neuro-degenerative diseases, including Alzheimer’s disease, dementia, Parkinson’s disease, and Lou Gehrig’s disease (ALS) are strongly related to exposure to environmental aluminum.

“Nanoparticles of aluminum are not only infinitely more inflammatory, they also easily penetrate the brain, including the blood and olfactory nerves. Studies have shown that these particles pass along the olfactory neural tracts, which connect directly to the area of the brain that is not only most effected by Alzheimer’s disease, but is also the earliest affected in the course of the disease. It also has the highest level of brain aluminum in Alzheimer’s cases.

"The intranasal route of exposure makes spraying of massive amounts of nanoaluminum into the skies especially hazardous, as it will be inhaled by people of all ages, including babies and small children. We know that older people have the greatest reaction to this airborne aluminum. Because of the nanosizing of the aluminum particles being used, home filtering systems will not remove the aluminum, thus prolonging exposure, even indoors."

He stared hard at the large rotund man who had asked the question. "Have you yourself sir, become aware of a lack of concentration? Have you found it difficult to focus or sleep recently?"

Everyone looked at Congressman Alleyne to see what his answer would be. Maybe he would not be able to keep his job if what was suggested proved to be true. They could see he was rattled.

He hesitated before replying. "But we here in DC are not affected, are we? There is no spraying in our skies. They do not spray in Brussels or other seats of government, do they?"

The scientist gave an ironic laugh. "Aren't you forgetting drift, winds, and so on?"

"But they are spraying a toxic cocktail of aluminum, strontium and barium from planes in a plot to control the weather, the population and our food supply. That is all to the good isn't it?"

"If that is that what you believe, then why are you concerned? Isn't population control the objective?" He abruptly closed his folder of journals, looked grimly at all present and sat down.

At this point everybody began to call out their opinions. The Chairman banged on the table for quiet, but the meeting collapsed into complete disarray. Everybody had forgotten why Colonel Adam Fenshawe was not present, all except the old General. He would investigate.

***

The Mothership buzzed with excitement. The word was that something was about to happen. Master M raised his arm so quickly that his robe fell back revealing his hand. Everyone there gasped at what they saw. His long spindly fingers glowed with such brilliance, as if a strong light was shining through them. They daren't look too long for their eyes became sore with the brightness. They quickly looked away as he gave them a sweet smile and quickly pulled the sleeve back over to cover the light.

"Maybe you now understand why I and others like me always wear robes," he said. "You could not withstand the brightness of our light. But enough of that, there is much to do. This Mothership must change its position, and preparation is needed. It is no longer hidden from Earth and attempts are being made to interfere and explore this Moon in a way that would be disastrous. Would you believe they intend to direct nuclear explosive weaponry at us yet again? They have already attempted this once before, but fortunately it was a long way from where we were situated at the time."

"Who are *they*?" Master M saw fear reflected in Jacob's eyes.

"They are those who wish to take over your beloved planet Earth and who have infiltrated the Shadow Government operating below your elected political radar. They also influence decisions made with NASA. I tell you that the majority of those even in the Shadow Government have no idea of the bigger picture, and truly believe that what they do is for the good of all. It is the minority within the group that you have to fear. They feel they are invincible and will not suffer the consequences of their actions. This is why they have so many tunnels all over the planet– but more of that later.

"So Jacob do not fear. All is in order. Those who have positive intent towards Earth have the advantage." Master M could see that Jacob was not convinced.

Jacob frowned as he reached out for Kate's hand. It was hard to believe that his daughter was Master M's granddaughter. Where did her future lie and where did he fit in to the picture? He sighed heavily.

"Tell me then, how you *knew* they were going to launch a nuclear device?" Jacob wanted more if he was to understand more fully.

Adam's head shot up smartly. "Do we tell them Master M?"

At that very moment they all felt a shudder. The entire room shook. It felt as if gravity had taken a brief holiday when all objects that were not fixed jumped up and then fell back.

"As I said, we need to move position. We are altering the gravitational field using counter rotating magnetics. This is just a preparation while we make the correct adjustments to the field." Master M issued an order to the attendant standing close by.

Adam repeated, "Do we tell them Master M?"

"This is not the time Adam, I must get you off this Mothership right now, and take Kate and her father with you. I am returning you all to Adam's apartment in DC. No arguments. Those against us will not expect that."

A light green mist began to engulf Adam, Kate and Jacob, but they felt nothing. Sechem and Jamère watched fascinated as they slowly disappeared.

"How did you do that?" Sechem asked.

Master M smiled. "I thought you knew by now my dear friend. In order for Jacob, Adam and Kate to be able to visit the Mothership, and to be here as long as they have, we had to temporarily bring the craft into a third density state for them. It served its purpose in making them comfortable while on board. But since we now have to move the entire Mothership to a different position it is necessary to change it into a higher dimension where it can dematerialise and be transported to its new location, and then later rematerialize if we wish. They cannot physically be here for this move."

"Of course. I see. They are in third dimensional form. They can only enter a higher consciousness state while in dreams or meditation trance," said Sechem.

"And that is not physical or static," Jamère added. "We adjust our densities all the time when we visit them, don't we?"

Master M stared hard at his team of time travellers. "You do not have the whole picture," he said. "It is not that they can't change their vibrational field along with the Mothership or stay longer, but it would not be good for their time spent on Earth. That is where they are meant to be, to do the job that is intended for them. They would have a hard time being in both places at once. That is why some psychics on the Earth plane have difficulty in staying grounded and their lives end up being a mess. They want to be with their spirit guides so much that they forget they were sent to do their work on Earth, not in the spirit realm. Else why go to Earth, why not stay where they were?"

"Good point," Sechem said.

Master M smiled. "Now let us get on with the move. We have wasted enough time."

CHAPTER TWO

NEW LOCATION

There is at times a need to take risks.
If you always take the safe route, then your life's
journey would become uneventful.
It would contain nothing extraordinary or worthy of notice.
Do you want your life to be like that?
If you do, then all well and good.
If not, then do not be afraid of the unknown.
This is where your trial of strength and purpose will be.

Kate was the first to appear in Adam's apartment. Next was Jacob who let out a groan of disappointment when he realised he was no longer on the Mothership with Master M. Kate looked around for Adam but couldn't see him. "Adam!" she yelled, her heart pounding. "Where are you?"

In another room Adam muttered to himself as he ruffled though the papers on his desk. "Damn, damn. Damn. Why can't I find my notes? I will need them if I am going to arrange accommodation. Where am I going to put them both that is safe? Master M has certainly put me in it this time. I need to find my maps and my security passes." He opened one drawer after another while still talking and grumbling to himself, "There's no room here in this tiny apartment, and they'll certainly be noticed by the concierge. A right mess you have put me into Master M, and it is up to you to fix it." He felt Kate's presence behind him and turned to face her.

"I'm glad you are back. Do you always talk to yourself?" she said grinning. "For once you don't have a clue what to do next, do you?" She felt calmer now that they were together. She hadn't forgotten how good it was to feel him holding her so tightly on the ship. She grabbed his arm and pulled him down onto a chair. "Sit. Take a breath; breathe deeply and calm down."

At that moment Jacob walked in. "What are we going to do next?" he asked. "Adam, it's all up to you now my lad."

Kate saw that Adam was rattled over the unexpected development and couldn't think straight. He was usually so organised and had it all in hand. Not this time. What had changed? She watched in alarm as he got up, staggered and nearly lost his balance. He swung round, arms outstretched, flailing around looking like a blind man trying to feel his way. It was time to call in help.

"Wherever you are Sechem and Jamère come quickly. We need you *now*."

Suddenly the television turned itself on, the screen scrambled and became fuzzy. "Oh Sechem, not more of your tricks this time, please. We need you."

"You called, my lady?" Sechem laughed, stepped out of the screen and did a twirl.

"Be serious Sechem. Can't you see how Adam is behaving? He's not himself at all. I'm very worried. What has caused this?"

Sechem watched for a moment or two at Adam lurching blindly around the room. He pulled him down onto a chair. "Before he injures himself," he said. "Hmm! Let me think. It must be Gork up to his tricks again."

A wail of despair went up from Jacob. Not that creature again? The same one that tried to freeze us all to death?"

"The very same." They all looked round to where the voice was coming from and recognised it as Jamère's.

"Show yourself Jamère." Jacob pleaded. "This is no time to fool around."

He began to take shape before them. They heard him snort. "I refuse to do the television trick Sechem uses. That is beneath me. Not much room in here though, is there?" he added as he looked around. "Now, let me see, Gork."

"Gork is still confined on the Mothership, isn't he?" Jacob asked, looking worried.

"First things first. Let's get Adam back to himself." Jamère grabbed hold of Adam's head and gave it a violent twist. "That should do it."

Adam gasped and fell forward. Jamère caught him and pushed him back onto the chair.

"What about Gork?" Kate said as Adam collected his wits. "Will we ever be safe from him?"

Jamère opened his mouth to speak, but Sechem stopped him. "What he is still capable of, even though he is confined, is using only his mind and his thoughts to affect others. Being imprisoned does not stop this. You should know this Kate when you had psychic attacks from Helga back in Dorset. Anybody can affect others by their thoughts and intentions. Let's hope they use them only with good intentions. They don't have to be ill meant as it is with Gork. A lot of healing can take place with the right thoughts."

Kate knew of many wonderful healers who sent healing energy remotely to those in need. She nodded and looked at Adam who was by now sitting up straight, alert, and clear eyed.

"I have decided," he said. "You and your father must stay here until I can arrange something else. We have no choice." Kate realised something else made him pause. His face reddened as he looked over at Jacob. "Would you mind if Kate and I shared my bed? You can have the couch."

Kate put her hand on her father's arm. "It's alright Dad, the couch is really comfortable I'm sure."

Jacob gave a slight nod of resignation. "Well, at least you can warn each other if Gork plays any more of his tricks. He won't come after me, after all I am not that important or a threat to him."

Sechem and Jamère quietly left the room.

***

Helga Mortenson and Silas Pearce made their way through the crowd at Dulles airport, Washington DC to the line-up of taxis. They had been summoned by the team that Silas hoped to join. It was the same group of men who always dressed in black, that Helga had hosted in her spacious home in Dorset. She was more than a little afraid of them and knew what they could do to her if she messed up. Kate had to be found and soon.

"It is no good your complaining about our accommodation Silas," she said as she thrust her luggage trolley through the crowds. "You would have preferred Bethesda I know, but it was booked for us and you know full well by whom." Helga sniffed the air. "It smells awful here. Why can't we go into a less congested area?"

"Maybe it is the chemicals from the spraying wafting their way into the buildings." Silas offered.

"Don't be ridiculous Silas. You realise they do not spray over DC." They got into a cab and went straight away to the meeting in the basement of an obscure building behind Capitol Hill. "Behave yourself there Silas. You know how ruthless they can be if you cross them."

Silas smiled to himself. "Yes, I know."

Inwardly Helga worried, remembering how coldly the steely faced man had treated her when he discovered she had not told him about her friendship with Kate Greene's mother Francine. She hoped he would not be present at the meeting.

***

That night in Adam's apartment everybody seemed at a loss as to what to do next. Adam realised he had to take charge, but his mind was going round and round getting nowhere. Then he remembered a message given to Kate by her unseen friends.

So many of you go round and round in circles and in doing so quite obviously see the same view as you revolve. Turn this circle into a spiral so that you are spun into new visions, new areas of understanding. An extra surge of desire or effort at any point in your circling will send you out of the ring that seems to bind you firmly.

As a satellite circling the Earth requires a booster rocket to project it into new areas, so you too need to fire your engines to break the pattern.

Yes, he had to act, and it had to be soon. Perhaps Kate was the boost he needed. He turned to her with an anxious look. Was she up to it after all that had happened? Would she be able to connect with her unseen world so soon? He had to ask, and after all she did have her special implant which allowed her to do many things others could not.

"Kate, do you think you could have one of your journeys? It might help us to understand what to do next. It's very soon I know, but your actions may give us an idea. We need to keep you safe."

He relaxed when he saw Kate's face light up at the request. He felt in his heart then that they would always be alright, but he needed reassurance of this.

She tossed her fair hair back. "Of course. I will try, but no guarantees of course. I never know what or who will come through. I will need your help, and Dad's too."

Jacob didn't look so sure. "What if they pick up on her energy signal Adam? That is how they tracked her before, isn't it?"

Kate patted his arm. "Oh don't be such a worrier Dad. It will be alright, but you will need to listen and take notes when I tell you what is happening. Just like before."

Adam's apartment was a typical bachelor's pad. He had the bare essentials but not much more. He very rarely socialised since he was out of the country so often and had no need for what others would consider necessary furnishings. Adam began arranging the few chairs he had so that they would be comfortable and would allow Kate to make her connections.

He looked around the room before dimming the lights. "Is everybody ready?"

Time seemed to slow down as both men watched Kate closely for signs that she had entered another world. Although they were well used to the process their mouths still dropped open in wonder when she began to disappear from her chair.

"Please speak to us Kate," Adam begged. "You know we can hear you. We are ready."

She began slowly and quietly at first, her words barely a whisper. Then it came with clarity.

"My steps are winding down a mountain side. The steps have been cut into the hillside, so they are natural, stones, wood, earth and whatever it takes to construct a foothold. I am on a mountain, it is open, no thick undergrowth or anything like that. There are lots of bends. I know it's the only way to get down the mountain safely. I am dressed in proper clothing for being outside. I have strong boots. I keep going down. It is not a high mountain, so it is not freezing. If anything, it's quite warm and is at a comfortable temperature. It's higher than the hills of Wales, but I am not on a really high mountain. I can hear the birds singing. I am at the bottom now and can see a flat grassy plain. There is a path. What have they done to my usual pattern of turn to the left, turn to the right? I have just got to follow the path to see where it goes.

"I come to what appears to be a large rounded hollow. It's not a crater and isn't deep. I go down a slope and wow, right at the bottom there's a space craft. It is typically round and slightly humming, buzzing, a vibrational humming. It feels inviting, that is how I feel about it. I walk closer to it. There's a rim all around it and as I get near I see the rim is wide enough to have windows. There are lights inside, it is very active. I don't know if I am meant to go into it or not. I'm walking closer and don't know what to do. As I walk around I'm looking for a door, which sounds ridiculous for I don't really expect to see any. Suddenly I find myself inside. I have no way of knowing how I got inside, but I am. It's as if the outer shell wasn't there and I just stepped through. No I didn't step. I simply found myself inside.

"It's amazing for it's like being in a different world but not as I would expect it to be like inside a craft. It is big here, alive. The interesting thing is that it is alive with nature such as you would have outside, greenery, bushes, and I feel there could be creatures here as well. So it is not mechanical inside, it is another country, another place. How odd! I had expected it to be a craft with machinery and instruments but there is none of that. I feel at home, which is a huge surprise to me. I feel I could walk for a long time and never reach the other edge.

"Two little creatures, humanoids about four feet tall come up to me. They are not Greys but have peachy coloured skin with a tinge of red to it. They're smiling and take my hands as they walk me along - - - long pause. Oh! I think I've crossed into another time, another place, another method of transport that you wouldn't expect. My mind is buzzing with the newness of this. The two peachy Greys look at me and I understand what they are thinking, no words. At this point I begin to speak their language. I can hear this in my head. I am in their land. I am in their time."

"I want to know where we are."

"You are on another civilisation's land mass."

"That doesn't tell me where I am."

"You are on another time frame, another existence." At this point more of their language came, but from them. "We are every bit as real as you. All you have done is break through from one time frame, that is to say from one area to another in space."

"They are trying to help me understand."

"It's a land mass on another cosmic body. We do not wish to use the word planet for that would not be quite accurate. We do not wish you to think of the cosmos as being composed only of planets and stars, for there are other land masses. Even the word land is incorrect. This is for you a new, existence, an ability to exist in any form. The land, and although that word is incorrect we use it for your sake only, land is a construction of your mind. It does not really exist in a physical sense."

"I am finding that hard because I am in third dimension and you, I can see you, hear and touch you."

"Yes, but you see you have not stepped outside the limiting frame of third dimensional thinking. You can be every bit a construct here as you are a construct on your planet Earth."

"I want to know; will I go back?"

"Of course you will go back. We will return you back. We just wished you to have an expansion of understanding of what you term reality. Reality is a difficult thing for you to understand. This *(experience)* is an intelligent mind construct. Even the word mind is incorrect for that incorrectly implies a physical brain. The mind does not have a brain. It exists in and of itself. It does not need a form but constructs a form to meet a specific request or occasion that requires the form for clarification. You could say that we do not exist except in your mind construct.

"That really has thrown me because I didn't deliberately construct you. Construct means, put together to construct something.

But this (*experience*) simply happened without me constructing it.

"You are forgetting that ***we*** have used our own mind construct and have included you within it. Are you happy with that?"

"I am perfectly happy with it. I know nothing can hurt me."

"That is the best way to view this for the only thing that can hurt you is yourself, your mind if you so wish, to be hurt. The rest is entirely up to you."

"I'm not afraid. I find it difficult to get my head around this."

"You will come to understand, for this will happen more and more. As we wish to show you things, we will construct the means to do this."

"Is this going to be of help to the planet Earth?"

Pause "This is a very large question."

"One I'd like an answer to."

"You see, we can construct things for you, but it is what you do with the information that comes with the construction of the mind that matters. It is again entirely up to you, or whoever receives this information."

A flash of knowing entered my mind. It concerned possible human habitation in the future. During this I saw that there would be choices as to how to live, depending on the prevailing environment. One choice was to live under domes, vast areas under cover. I am reminded of the Eden Project in Cornwall. Another choice was to live under the sea. There would be long tunnels leading to undersea cities. I believe something like this already exists but is secret.

"Is this a construct of my mind too?" I ask them without getting a reply.

"It is time for you to go. It is time for you to go back."

"Whew! I find I am standing outside this – I can't call it a spaceship – apparatus, mind construct? I am standing outside it now, as me, quite happy."

As Adam and Jacob listened and recorded her words, they

longed to have had the experience for themselves. Kate slowly re-materialised in her chair until they could see her clearly again.

Adam was the first to speak. "That was marvellous Kate. You make it seem so easy, but then you also have the implant."

"Desire and intention is all that is needed my darling. Oh, and of course the ability to meditate to a deep level. That's all that is required." Kate yawned. "Anything to eat?"

***

In a secluded back street off Capitol Hill in Washington DC, a group of serious men with stern faces stood around in clusters to discuss the absence of their leader Gork. They had previously experienced being plunged into terrifying visions of hell when looking into Gork's eyes. Thankfully he had worn very dark glasses all of the time, knowing he would not get much done by anyone being traumatised on seeing his eyes.

The small knot of men standing by the window surrounded an enormous newcomer. This was Valdek, whose reputation as being formidable, preceded him.

Some had heard he was even more terrible than Gork. Although human in form his build was bulkier than any human. His thick neck supported a square head covered by heavy coils of hair. His eyes were narrow, like slits. He wore a thick heavy coat down to his knees. They were all thankful that he had no need of dark glasses. They relaxed, just a little.

Due to Gork, the terrible one's non-appearance at the meeting, the aging General decided that as he was the most senior and respected person there he was the one expected to take over.

He moved to the head of the table, tapped his glass with his baton to draw attention. He began the proceedings. "Please be seated. We must not wait any longer as obviously Gork is not going to come." He noticed that the new man Valdek proceeded to take Gork's usual seat at the table. A ripple of surprise and interest spread along the table. The General gave a gruff cough, more to bring attention back to him than anything else, but all eyes were fixed on Valdck.

"Before we do anything else, we must talk about and track down Colonel Adam Fenshawe. For this reason I have commanded that Silas Pearce and Helga Mortensen be present at this meeting. They have had many close interactions with him in his business dealings and are more likely to know where he is and possibly predict his movements. I have taken the liberty of bringing them both to our headquarters.

He signalled to the soldier standing guard by the door. "Bring them in."

A murmur of disapproval could be heard through the room which the old man did not miss. He realised it was an unpopular move to bring civilian outsiders into what was principally a deeply secret military team, but it was his best chance to bring the young Colonel down. He had made it his mission since the meeting months before when the whippersnapper challenged him over the use of Jump Rooms and available places for time travel. The old man was determined that the team would choose his young grandson and saw Fenshawe as the obstacle to that.

The door flung open so violently it hit the soldier guarding the door in the face. Helga marched into the room followed by Silas. "There had better be a good reason for dragging us all the way from England," she stormed.

Silas shrank back horrified. This was no way to get invited to join this powerful team of men.

"Madam, control yourself. Don't you know whom you are addressing?" The old General growled, ready to explode in anger. This was not what he expected from those he considered to be inferior participants in the drive to keep Kate Greene's nose out of their business. "Please sit down and calm yourself."

Helga and Silas crossed the room and took seats placed strategically at the far end of the table. As he watched their expressions, he could see it was not going to be as easy as he had hoped. "Now, tell us how you expect to find Kate Greene and her father." He drummed his fingers on the table signalling impatience. "And what do you know of Colonel Adam Fenshawe?"

As he said this a loud and harsh voice interrupted the questioning. The old General unhappily knew at once he had to bow to the superiority of Commandant Valdek after all.

With your permission, General, "I will take charge of this. This is *my* business, not yours."

The old General's keen eyes noticed how the woman's face blanched, and he swore she trembled with the overwhelming power of the man who was taking charge. Silas Pearce appeared to enjoy her discomfort, and he wondered at it.

Although the General was taken aback, he said, "Yes, yes, of course sir. And you have met them before I understand." The old man waved his arm in a way that indicated 'over to you'.

The giant man's face showed contempt as he looked at Helga with red steely eyes. "What have you discovered so far?"

"Kate and her father seem to have vanished off the face of the Earth," she said, "and all our efforts to locate them have been in vain. We were hoping that you would have better luck."

"Luck, luck?" his enraged shout rang through the room sending shivers of alarm over those attending. His voice abruptly turned icy and deadly soft. The old General sensed threat and wondered if Valdek could be even worse than Gork.

"I'll tell you now that we do not operate on luck. We have *other* means."

The General saw that the threat in his voice had sent dread

through Helga, but the General also noticed fascination and even admiration all over Silas's face. It was at that precise moment he thought he saw a dark shadow figure move slowly across the room to stand before Valdek. It appeared to be waiting.

"Meanwhile, you Helga will use your own psychic senses and attempt to pick up her energy signature, just in case she tries to get into our secure facilities again." Helga breathed a heavy sigh of reprieve. "You, Pearce, come with me, *now*." He got up from the table and with Silas tagging along like a faithful dog they left the room, much to the old General's relief. He could now get on with the business of Adam Fenshawe. Where the devil was he?

CHAPTER THREE

IN HIDING

Underneath this reality in which we live and have our being,
another and altogether different reality lies concealed.
– Friedrich Nietzsche

Jacob paced up and down Adam's apartment. The sofa wasn't uncomfortable, but he yearned for his own bed. He wondered, not for the first time, if he was strong enough and brave enough to handle what could lie ahead. Were they ever going to be safe and free to do whatever they wanted to do? Would they ever go back to living a normal life? What would happen if they were discovered in Adam's apartment? And most worrying of all, where were Sechem and Jamère when they were needed? It was 3.00 am and he could hear the gentle breathing from the other room of his beloved daughter sleeping beside Adam. How he envied them and longed to be with his own love Joslene, so far away. He lay down again and eventually dropped off to a sleep full of dreams and nightmares.

***

Next morning a tousle headed Kate went into the sitting room and pulled the covers off her father. She bent over to give him a soft kiss on his head. "Wake up sleepy head."

Adam appeared in the doorway smiling all over and with a bounce in his step.

"What shall we have for breakfast? We have a lot to work out this morning," he said with such energy in his voice that Jacob took heart again. All would be well, and he was worrying over nothing. They would be protected, wouldn't they?

Adam watched Jacob and saw his worried expression as he ate his breakfast and knew he had to calm him if his plan was to work.

"Jacob, last night Kate and I came to an agreement which I hope you will like."

Jacob stopped eating immediately and looked over at Kate like an anxious child seeking reassurance.

"Tell me," he said.

"As you may realise, that in my position and with a good income I have another property, apart from this apartment, which I use just to be near my work. It is a legacy from the original Colonel Fenshawe. You and Kate can move in there. They wouldn't in a million years dream you would go there. It is closed up now but could easily be opened again and it has no bugs or connection with my colleagues."

Jacob brightened. "If you think you can get us there without being discovered then I am all for it," he said.

"Don't worry about that, my friend. It is already being taken care of. You forget I also have friends within the Shadow Government."

"You do? How come?"

Adam paused before answering. Jacob realised he didn't want to say too much at this point. "Well, let us just say the cracks are showing and some members are having doubts about their role in what they do and what they know. They can see that it has all got out of control. Even they realise they cannot escape the consequences of drought, fire and floods and are worried about how it will affect their own families. As I said, the cracks are showing. They are beginning to understand that they are not immune to the negative effects of chemtrails and the use of the HAARP array (*High Frequency Active Auroral Research Program*) that is said to modify the weather. It is also said HAARP was to be dismantled and shut down in 24 May 2014. I don't know if it really was closed because the ionospheric research station in Gakona at the University of Alaska Fairbanks took it over from the Air Force in 2015. I suspect they are moving on to other ways of managing the ionosphere, for which the HAARP was really designed. Weather warfare is not a thing of the past Jacob and may continue to play a role in warfare. My concern is that Europeans built five HAARP type arrays and subsequently earthquakes began happening nearby."

Jacob started to look worried again and a frown appeared on his face. "How are people on Earth going to survive all the upheaval that climatic change brings, to say nothing of chemicals in our food and skies?"

Kate moved swiftly to her father and turned him to face her. "Now look here Dad, you know we are on a good path to a better future. Why would all those wonderful new children be coming to Earth to give us a hand? They wouldn't come if they thought it was a lost cause. And how about all the amazing people who are caring and doing such wonderful work? That is not going to waste either. As Adam has told you, the cracks are showing in those who take part in the Shadow Government. More and more whistle-blowers are coming forward too. For goodness sake, have more faith in the Human Race."

Jacob looked sheepish. "I know, I know my darling girl, but it has all been a bit too much for me in such a short time. I don't know if I can cope with much more."

None of them noticed the dark shadow move across the room, but they all felt the icy cold blast that came with it.

***

Jacob slept well that night but knew he had to explain something to his daughter before anything could arrive and worry her unnecessarily. He didn't want her to be unprepared, as she was when she met the Black Goo. He had seen the Shadow that had crossed the room the day before. Did his daughter see it too but decided not to say anything? He had to be sure. It had brought back memories of the Shadow Being that came to him in the garden in Tadley while he was mowing the grass. It did not seem unfriendly, and it turned out that it had only come to warn him. Jacob frowned, was this the same Shadow or another, not so friendly? If he explained what Shadow People were to Kate maybe she could intuit whether the latest one to show was well intentioned or not.

They ate breakfast together and Adam set off for his office. A little time passed before he felt able to broach the subject.

"Kate, my darling, could we have a little chat?"

She frowned, was he going to worry about nothing again? "Of course Dad. It is good to talk. Let's go into the garden."

He had to start. "Kate, what do you know about shadows?"

Kate laughed. "Dad, you silly, of course I do. I am not a child. Why do you ask?"

"There are many kinds of shadows. Did you know that there is a race of Cosmic beings called The Shadow People?"

"You are having me on," she laughed. "How can a shadow be a person?"

"Listen Kate, I had one visit me in Tadley. We communicated telepathically."

"OK, you have got my attention. Tell me more. Why did it go to you? You didn't tell me. Why not?"

"I was an energy source for it at the time. It took what energy it needed and in return gave me a message. It is not important now what the message was. But you do need to know about them for they may visit you as an energy source. They are not good or bad, but they are inquisitive. They like to learn and make use of the energy coming from Humans, especially when human emotions are high, either positive or negative. They are only interested in energy, nothing else. They do not like being near groups of people who are united in thought and feelings, mainly because those groups are usually peaceful, and their energy is not what they call 'red'."

"Why are you telling me, Dad if they are harmless?" Kate was puzzled.

"You have high energy, a good source for them. They may attach to you and you would not know it. Should you see or feel them they *will* leave you if you ask them to go. You only have to ask them to go. When they are not being Shadows they do have a physical body which is not frightening. They have dark hair and colouring and only become shadows when they wish to travel in their search for energy."

Kate furrowed her brow again. "Should I be worried, Dad? If they are not harmful or dangerous, why tell me?"

"You might see one and not know how to react. They look human in shape, usually tall and very dark. If you get emotional, fearful or angry and so on, they may attach for the energy that produces. You may also need to pass this information on to others. I doubt if they will bother you since you are generally calm, serene and peaceful, which will not produce the red energy they like."

"Wow! Dad that was a lot to take in but thank you for telling me. It could be useful in the future." She gave him a kiss on his head and together they sat and pondered.

***

Adam left the two together after reassuring them that their move to his house was all in hand. An urgent call from one of his trusted colleagues had to be dealt with.

“Where on earth have you been? You have to get over here damn quick if you want to avoid trouble,” the caller said, and cut the line.

Fifteen minutes later Adam was shown into the General’s well-appointed office. As he entered, he couldn’t help but notice the many photos of the General in active service and his proudly displayed medals. He also saw photos of the General’s only son who was killed in action, and several of his grandson in full uniform.

“You are in trouble young man. We have been trying to contact you.”

Adam gulped. He had to think quickly. His usual patter of, ‘it’s secret and I am not allowed to say,’ wouldn’t work this time. He pasted a look of contrite apology on his face as he stood before the old man. “I am so sorry sir, but on my travels I fell in love with the most wonderful girl - - - you know how it is?”

“No I do not know how it is,” the General growled. “Explain it to me.”

Adam put on a silly grin as he imagined how a lovesick man would look. *I’m getting good at this acting,* he thought to himself.

“Well Sir, I didn’t expect it to happen, but it did, and it has thrown all my usual common sense out of the window. I completely forgot to inform anyone that I had missed my plane and was stuck in the UK.”

“Wait up there. What has this got to do with you not responding to my calls?”

Still thinking on his feet Adam said, “We were trying to get seats for all of us on the same plane.” Immediately he realised his mistake. He had gone too far in concocting his story. The General was quick off the mark.

“We? All of us? What do you mean, all of us? Explain yourself, or it will be the worst for you, irrespective of your special security status." Adam saw satisfaction at that idea written all over the General's stern face. Was that a smirk he saw there?

"Sir, I waited to tell you about my private life until I was sure she reciprocated my feelings. Now I am sure. We want to get married." Adam watched the old man's reaction as this news sank in. But would it ease the situation and let him off the hook?

Adam breathed again when he saw the General smiling warmly at him. "Why didn't you say so my boy? We always wondered why such a good-looking young man was not in a relationship. We all thought you might be gay. Not that there is anything wrong with that," he added hastily.

"Well sir, with your permission I'd like them to stay with me at my house until we can arrange the wedding."

"Hold on there son, who is we? Who else is coming over? I need to know if I am to arrange clearance, papers etc." Adam saw fluster creeping up on the General's face.

"Sorry, sir. It's her father. She won't leave him behind, and he is the only family she has. Oh, and then there is the mother, but I don't expect her to come too."

"Oh, I see. Well let me have the details of all of them and I will get it sorted. Close the door on your way out."

The meeting was over and Adam left feeling relieved, but at the same time he was puzzled. Why the change of heart from the old man? Was that all an act?

CHAPTER FOUR

NEW RESIDENCE

The real voyage of discovery consists not in seeking new landscapes but in having new eyes. Marcel Proust

Kate woke up early. She could hear the birds singing outside in the small garden and she felt at peace. Adam was due to return shortly and would show her around Bethesda and its famous Mushroom House, but she still wondered at the continued absence of Jamère and Sechem. Where were they and why hadn't they helped at all over the panic of the last few days? For the first time she began to worry about them. Perhaps the Mothership's move to a new location had gone wrong after all. Perhaps a nuclear weapon from Earth had been able to track them. She was acutely aware that many amateur and professional astronomers were watching the Moon carefully and were picking up strange objects on the surface with their telescopes. If they only knew what was going on inside the Moon too, they would be so surprised. Should she tell the world, or should she keep quiet?

Kate remembered very clearly how she had been taken into the Moon's interior and met the people living inside, whole families who were afraid of the activities of the military forces on Earth. They were right to be worried. Kate knew from her research that Milton Cooper, a Naval Intelligence Officer said that not only does an Alien Moon Base exist on the far side of the Moon but the U.S. Naval Intelligence Community refers to the Alien Moon Base as “Luna,” that there is a huge mining operation going on there, and that is where the aliens keep their huge mother ships while the trips to Earth are made in smaller “flying saucers”. During her visit to the Moon’s interior she was told that the Moon did indeed have an atmosphere about three miles thick. This was proven by astronomers M K Jessup and V A Firsoff. She was told that the Moon have mists, clouds and fogs and the most precious of all, water. The family she met within the Moon laughed at the attempts to cover this up during the second visit by astronauts. The flags they planted were rigged with wires and mesh so that they remained rigid.

Kate was deeply concerned in knowing all this information. Since the psychic watchers for the Shadow Government seemed to know so much perhaps her own visits to the Mothership were also seen and recorded.

Through her research Kate had read that both Neil Armstrong and Edwin “Buzz” Aldrin saw UFOs shortly after their historic landing on the Moon in Apollo 11 on 20 July 1969. One of the astronauts referred to a “light” in or on a crater during their television transmission, followed by a request from mission control for further information.

This was their recorded transmission, not open to the public of course:

NASA: What’s there? Mission Control calling Apollo 11...

Apollo: These “Babies” are huge, Sir! Enormous! OH MY GOD! You wouldn’t believe it! I’m telling you there are other spacecraft out there, lined up on the far side of the crater edge! They’re on the Moon watching us!

In 1979, Maurice Chatelain, former chief of NASA Communications Systems confirmed that Armstrong had indeed reported seeing two UFOs on the rim of a crater. *“The encounter was common knowledge in NASA,"* he revealed, *"but nobody has talked about it until now."*

So the public were still held in ignorance, Kate realised. Perhaps she should enlighten them after all? She knew that Soviet scientists were allegedly the first to confirm the incident. *"According to our information, the encounter was reported immediately after the landing of the module,"* said Dr. Vladimir Azhazha, a physicist and Professor of Mathematics at Moscow University. Neil Armstrong relayed the message to Mission Control that two large, mysterious objects were watching them after having landed near the Moon module. But his message was never heard by the public-because NASA censored it.

According to another Soviet scientist, Dr. Aleksandr Kazantsev, Buzz Aldrin took movie film of the UFOs from inside the module, and continued filming them after he and Armstrong went outside. Dr. Azhazha claims that the UFOs departed minutes after the astronauts came out on to the lunar surface.

Before she could pass any of this to the public Kate realised she needed to think carefully. But then again, isn't this what she was supposed to do? If she came forward she could be at risk just by revealing the truth about UFOs and alien Moon bases.

So why did NASA eventually terminate the Apollo missions if extra-terrestrial visitors were there and watching the Earth? The answer according to Armstrong at a NASA symposium is as follows:

Professor: *What really happened out there with Apollo 11?*

Armstrong: *It was incredible ... of course, we had always known there was a possibility ... the fact is, we were warned off. There was never any questions then of a space station or a Moon city.*

Professor: *How do you mean "warned off"?*

Armstrong: *I can't go into details, except to say that their ships were far superior to ours both in size and technology – Boy, were they big! ... and menacing .... No, there is no question of a space station.*

Professor: *But NASA had other missions after Apollo 11?*

Armstrong: *Naturally – NASA was committed at that time and couldn't risk a panic on Earth.... But it really was a quick scoop and back again.*

Kate decided it needed more thought. The Spiritual Galactic Confederation had constrained Gork so she assumed her friends would be safe from him. Then with a jolt she remembered how Gork had used his mind to deliberately put her in danger. She shivered despite the warmth of the house.

She heard her father moving about downstairs and hoped he had calmed down and was his dependable self once more. It was time to see how he was doing. On entering the kitchen Kate was delighted to see him tucking into a large plate of food. "I see you have made yourself at home," she said laughing and planted a kiss on his head.

"I don't know how he does it. Adam has so much else on his mind and yet he looks after us so well. My hat off to him," Jacob said between mouthfuls of food.

"Adam does his best and it is important to us both that you are happy, Dad. What would we do without you?" She looked at him and smiled. "Dad, you are dribbling." Kate chuckled as she leant forward to wipe his chin.

"I am not much use though, am I? I panic when it gets rough. What is the good in that?"

"Dad, you silly man. I could not continue without your stabilising presence."

"What is this all about?" neither of them had noticed Adam as he entered the kitchen. "Now let's get down to business and decide what we are going to do next."

Kate watched his face carefully. Was that excitement she saw there?

Adam sat down facing them across the table. He whispered quietly into her ear. "Do you remember Kate when I asked you an important question?"

"Yes I do, and I never got a chance to answer before we were interrupted."

Adam sighed. "Since then there hasn't been an opportunity to - - -. Jacob, would you mind if we left you for a bit?"

Jacob looked down at his plate of food. "No, of course I don't mind. Carry on."

Adam grabbed Kate's hand and pulled her into the other room and shut the door firmly behind him.

"Yes, Adam? What is this all about?"

At that precise moment a flash of bright blue light filled the room, dazzling them. When their eyes adjusted they saw both Jamère and Sechem standing close to each other by the window.

Sechem did one of his little jigs. "What he is trying to tell you is that you are to be married." He and Jamère held hands and danced around each other.

Adam was furious. "You might have given me the chance to propose and get a reply. You are insufferable."

"Yes," added Jamère. "your timing is really off Sechem my friend."

Kate was silent throughout until she couldn't hold back any longer. "It sounds to me as if you have it planned and buttoned up already." Bemused, she stared at Adam.

Adam turned to the two Time Travellers. "Now, be quiet you two. That is if you ever could."

He got down on one knee in front of his love.

Adam's voice shook as he asked. "Kate, my darling. Will you honour me by being my wife?"

The two men began clapping. The stern look on Adam's face stopped them. "For goodness sake, give her time to answer." He looked at Kate with such an anxious expression that Kate loved him even more.

"Of course I will," she said. "I've been dreaming about this Adam, but how can I be your wife given your position within the Shadow Government?"

At that moment Jacob walked in. "What's all the commotion?" Then he saw Sechem and Jamère by the window and Adam in the act of getting up from kneeling. His jaw dropped. Grinning he embraced Kate and shook Adam's hand. Then he turned on the men, furious with them. "Where have you been? We really needed you here. Fine friends you turned out to be."

"Easy does it, old man. You know we are only here when there is work to be done, not just to calm your nerves."

"Old man? You cheeky so and so," Jacob frowned. "Hey, what work? When?"

"Now," they said together. "Right now. Let's get ready. Explanations and all the rest can wait. Someone important wants to speak to Kate."

Together they began to gather the chairs and put them in position. Would this be a task they would do collectively, or would it be just Kate? So much was happening, and nothing seemed to remain the same for long.

***

A group of dark suited men gathered in a small room just off the main corridor of a hotel on Capitol Hill. They had responded to an unusual summons from secret governmental headquarters and everyone seemed to be unnaturally nervous. The old General kept his feelings to himself but was on edge too. He knew this was not their normal venue for their meetings and that the men were sensing that something was afoot, maybe out of their control. This they did not like. He watched and waited as they shuffled their feet and eyed each other up. Did anyone there know what the call was for and what were they keeping quiet? The old man coughed loudly. It was becoming a habit whenever he was unsure of his ground. As a man used to controlling many men under his command it was a pattern he did not want to recognise in himself.

Suddenly the door was flung open with such force that it jolted them all out of their thoughts. As a body they all tried to avert their eyes when an impressive figure strode in. However it was not the horrific Gork whom they had half expected: who appeared was his replacement Valdek and who was equally, if not more frightening.

Valdek's bloodshot red eyes watched their every move. In spite of their important positions within the Shadow Government they felt fear. His expression was menacing. As the General returned his stare his heart beat painfully in his chest. He felt he was tumbling into an abyss.

Valdek was not alone. Two figures he had met earlier trotted into the room before the door closed again. Silas led the way with Helga following close behind.

Valdek nodded to them. "Sit down all of you." It was clear to the General that Valdek was again in charge and that it was he who had ordered the meeting. Was this going to be about Time Travelling machines at last? His disappointment came fast at Valdek's next words.

"I have called you here to tell you it is vital to dispel rumours among the general public that there is an invisible government, sometimes called the Deep State. They *must* not know that we exist. Some of you are becoming slack, and it will not be tolerated." Valdek flung copies of a report across the table. "Read this, all of you."

Helga and Silas along with the men, sat to read the report in silence.

Quote:

Even to this day, if people say there is an invisible government, or a shadow government that's international, they may call you a conspiracy theorist or give you a funny look.

This is in large part due to the lack of education, particularly self-education, of a population who is trained to go to school, get a job and 'enjoy' life. Sure, that's all well and good, but to deny and condemn a thought or an idea without any investigation is definitely the height of ignorance. Not only is it the height of ignorance, it also prevents humanity from moving forward. In order for us to move forward, we must properly identify our problems, and it doesn't help when the most important problems that need to be identified are not even believed as a result of mass brainwashing and lack of education. No one is thinking for themselves, instead they simply rely on establishment media, which has been nothing but a massive propaganda machine since its inception.

The idea of a shadow government doesn't only come from statements made by a number of global politicians and 'world leaders,' it's been proven by policy changes and decisions that are not in favour of the people or the planet, which expose how our federal regulatory agencies are run by rogue interests. Political parties no longer serve the people, and it's hard to say if they ever really did. Government and politics are now simply, as President Theodore Roosevelt emphasized, "tools of corrupt interests which use them in martialling to serve their selfish purposes." He flat out stated that "Behind the ostensible government sits enthroned an invisible government owing no allegiance and acknowledging no responsibility to the people. To destroy this invisible government, to befoul the unholy alliance between corrupt business and corrupt politics is the first task of the statesmanship of the day."

This is the unseen power that exists today. Roosevelt wasn't the only one, in his farewell speech President Eisenhower warned about the rise of misplaced power that exists and will persist within the military industrial complex.

Not long ago, President Vladimir Putin explained how, after a president in the United States is elected, "men in dark suits" come in and basically run the show. According to President Woodrow Wilson:

End Quote:

The reading continued in silence interrupted by an occasional embarrassed cough. Each person there acutely aware of the menacing figure that prowled behind them and Helga and Silas as they read, adding to the tension in the air. The General was painfully aware of beads of sweat forming uncomfortably under his collar. Eventually, one after the other they looked up from the report. Nobody spoke. Valdek walked threateningly around the room, behind the seated men and Helga and Silas. The General tensed and waited for what Valdek might do or say next. He did not have long to wait.

"Enough!" They all jumped in their seats. "This kind of reporting must be stopped."

The menace that came with those words sent a shiver of fear through the old man. He wondered and not for the first time, what he had got himself into. All he had ever wanted was for his grandson to be a time travelling chrononaught.

"What I want to know is how did this article come to light and be passed round the Internet? I'll tell you how. That, that woman Kate Greene is the reason. Not only does she go where it is secret, but she is spreading what she discovers to all and sundry. She must be stopped." These last words came in a high-pitched shriek.

The General put his hands over his ears. "Sir." He blinked nervously. "Sir, I know where she is."

Valdek swung round, fury on his face. Everyone held their

breath. Then he said in such a quiet menacing voice reminding the General of a snake about to strike.

"Where? Where is she?" he hissed.

"Bethesda." His voice shook. "She is going to marry Colonel Adam Fenshawe."

Out of the corner of his eye he saw Silas and Helga twitch with excitement.

"Excellent." Valdek surprised them all with that reaction. "We will be able to keep an eye on them there at last. They can't put their noses where they are not wanted without us knowing."

"Sir?" Helga raised her hand. "Could Silas and I be tasked with keeping an eye on Kate Greene and her father? We already know them well and have worked with Gork regarding their activities."

Valdek snorted. "Gork, useless creature! Well he paid the price for overstepping the rules of the Confederation. Since I am not going to continue belonging to the Confederation, I do not have to follow their stupid rules much longer."

The General felt a chill come over him and he shivered. What did that mean? He began to wonder again if he was right in being with this group of people. His attention wandered to the body of a dead fly on the carpet. He felt a sudden pity for it, and wondered how it came to be lying there, almost a mere smudge on the floor. One moment with its own purpose, and now insignificant. He drifted in thought, musing on the chance circumstance of its death, the futility of life. Lost in his reverie he did not notice Helga and Silas sidle up to Valdek. They were in deep conversation with him when he came back to his senses, aroused by a pungent smell of sulphur that hung in the room.

CHAPTER FIVE

THE OVERSEER SPEAKS

Present man is dying and will dic when the ice melts. Current man knows and accepts he is dying by degrees and that Mother Earth is killing him. She is waiting for the ice to melt. When it does he will die and she will give birth to new man.

There was not much time for celebration over Kate and Adam's engagement. Jacob bustled around getting chairs in place for Kate's next adventure into the unknown. Where would she go next? Who was the important person who wanted to meet her? Adam and Jacob sat on the edge of their seats. Sechem and Jamère appeared to be on edge too, for as usual nobody really knew what might happen or where Kate would be taken.

"As before Kate, speak to us throughout so we don't lose you." Adam said.

But Kate was already fading from their sight into a golden blur. She began to speak.

"I am in a tight, close-fitting silver suit. The stairs I go down on are metal, pure metal, nothing else, no wood, nothing but silvery metal. I make no sound as I go and my feet feel as if they are padded, not like hard shoes. Everything is soft, everything flows seamlessly as if in a river of silver mercury, flowing from one thing to the other as I go.

"I am muttering to myself. Muttering is not quite the right word. I am reciting something to myself as I go. I don't understand it, but I imagine it's some sort of language. All the way down I chant, a speaking of some kind. It's as if this is part of what is to happen next, preparation for entry into new worlds. Sounds, seamless, no effort, no mechanical means, everything flows.

"I am where I'm meant to be at the beginning of a journey. As I look ahead the landscape is not clearly defined and seems to merge with everything. There are creatures, all kinds of creatures popping up here and there, as if they come out of the merging, simply to show themselves."

A voice speaks. "The creatures of the past and creatures of the future are here together. Do not be concerned about the vanishing of some species, of your animals, for they are not lost, since their DNA and their journeys continue. They do not have to be where you can see them or experience them in a third dimensional world. It does mean that they continue as in their various species elsewhere, and into the future. Some will reincarnate into higher forms. They are not lost at all. They have merely moved from one density to another. As various species disappear from your planet through the actions of man, or for other reasons, they reappear elsewhere. There is no death.

"There is no death of any species. Everything continues and maybe have changes. This is true also for the Human Race. Even if, and we hope this does not happen, but even if the Human Race were to end on the planet Earth they too will resurface in another dimension, or world, or state of being. There is no death. Nothing that has existed ceases to be. All continues in one form or another, modified or not. There are also divisions when they resurface. They may divide in the way that cells divide and move along in their existence in a slightly altered form. This is to enable them to survive in whatever climate situation, or state they find themselves in. There may be modifications, no, there ***will*** be modifications of the Human Race."

"I want to know, will they come back to Earth in this dimension or another?"

"They will come back to Earth, but there is more than one Earth. They choose what would be most comfortable for them, to return either to your current third dimension Earth, or another altered, adjusted, adapted Earth. There are many alternatives to choose from. So you see the Human Race will not cease to exist, but may be adapted, adjusted for its own comfort and growth."

"Thank you. Who am I speaking to?"

"The Overseer of Human Souls."

"Overseer? What does that mean?"

"Each race, each species, whatever it may be, has what we would call an Overseer, someone who watches, monitors, records, takes notes and makes some adjustment where necessary. The Overseer also protects when it is deserved. We feel you are struggling for a name for me. I am The Overseer, you might call it the Divine Source, the God Force, or all the various names your separate religions have given, so many over the years. There is an Overseer for each Universe.

"You are probably right now in your mind trying to put a visual form over the concept of an Overseer. If this helps you to understand that this is perfectly natural. However, it is not a One Being, but an intelligence all of its own, that feels responsibility for its particular branch of existence. We call it The Overseer; you will give it other names which may suit you better. Your brains have not yet advanced enough to understand the greater worlds or the enormity of existence throughout many Universes, not just your own."

Adam clearly heard Sechem give a grunt at this. He wondered how much did Sechem really know as a Time Traveller. He knew that we are all time travellers really. He brought his attention back to what was coming through Kate's mouth.

She asked, "If we continue in the way we are, what is the future of the Human Race?"

"Have we not just told you that if, and it is always in your hands, if the Human Race destroys its habitable world so that it cannot exist on its home planet Earth, the Human Race will continue. Have we not already told you that? It may resurface into an environment that it can be comfortable with, that it can endure, that it can enjoy. There is such a variety of choices for the Human Race. If it ceases to exist on your current, and we stress the word current, planet Earth, that is, the state of being that it is currently in. There have been times before, there will be phases yet again. So you see, the future of the Human Race is variable. We say it is also varied for each individual soul, not just the race as a whole. Try to get your head round that."

"What is the purpose of the journey of the human being?" Kate asked.

"The purpose of every soul that has ever existed, that will ever exist, the purpose is to return to Source. By that we do not mean to The Overseer but beyond The Overseer, much greater. Inbuilt is that desire to return. It may not be aware, but that is the ultimate purpose."

Jamère saw that Jacob had fallen asleep and was glad that Adam was recording everything as Kate continued.

"He finishes talking and I'm standing in an environment of flowing movement. I see there are several different directions I can go. They're hard to define because they flow into each other on all sides but there still appears to be a direction in different ways. I wonder which one do I take. Then I see over to the right, I have the sense of wanting to go there for no particular reason. It has a stronger pull to it. I move along to it, though I can't call it a channel, for everything is so seamless here.

The voice continued. "You have just learnt a lesson."

"What's that?"

"Where you go is dependent on the pull a certain way has for you. If only all were to listen and take note of the pull within them to do this or that. Go with that. I can hear you say *There are many pulls, and we never know which one to go with, so many choices. Do we do this, or do we do that? We do not know. We really have no idea which is the best one."*

"The one that puts a smile on your face is the one you go towards. The one that makes you feel warm and glad. Ignore all others."

"Some might say that is self-serving."

"Isn't that what the journey is about? To serve, the journey of the Self."

"But some would say that is selfish."

"What you are forgetting is that giving help to others, solving a problem for others, doing what you can to assist others, these are the very things that give a warming of the heart, a glad feeling in knowing you are loved; these are the things that make you smile. We are not saying that everything that makes you warm is the most comfortable or the easiest route. We often find that it is the most difficult route that gives you the smile, for the satisfaction and the glow that it brings to you."

"This is all very deep for me."

"Yes, but there will be others who understand exactly what we are saying. There will also be those who do not agree and who do not understand. That is how it has always been throughout the ages."

"I feel gratitude for this experience as it fades from my mind. I have been here in mind only."

Jacob stirred as Kate began to reform in her chair. She rubbed her eyes, a sign that she was becoming conscious again. Jacob too revived sufficiently to welcome her back.

"How was it, Kate? What happened? Did I miss anything?"

"Darling father," she said. "did you go to sleep again?"

***

In the hotel room Helga sat quietly thinking. Silas looked on without disturbing her. What was she hatching up now? Was he to be included in her plans or left out in the cold? Neither of them had received any orders from Valdek since the last meeting. It left him uneasy. Was he to be included in the team or not?

Suddenly Helga gave a shout. "That's what we will do," she said, excited now.

"What will we do?" he asked. At least she had used 'we' instead of I. He was to be included after all. He breathed again. "What have you in mind?" he asked.

"We will call in the Orbs. They will give us any information we need."

"Excuse me?" Silas had no idea what she was talking about. "The Orbs? How can they help?"

"You know nothing." Silas squirmed under her scornful look. "I have been told that the Orbs can collect and supply information if asked. As I understand it if you need information, you call in the Orbs using your mind. They will come, and you tell them what you want to know. They never know it there and then, but if you ask them to go off and get the information and bring it back, they will. I understand they absorb energy and information, any information, good or bad. They are attracted to low frequency sounds and will draw near where there is sound. But although they carry so much information, they have no emotions at all. Think of them as a big reference book. I don't know if any of this is true or not, but it is worth a try, don't you think?"

Silas was doubtful. "How could we interpret what they might give us? What if they do not want to give us information?"

Helga frowned. "Well I understand that they do not hold humans in high esteem. They think we have messed things up big time, especially to do with Earth cycles and the rhythm of the Earth. We change one thing and cause another disastrous change which is not to Earth's advantage. For example look at the way HAARP operates to change the ionosphere and adjust the weather cycles. Floods, droughts, hurricanes, causing the disappearance of whole species of creatures, to name just a small amount of damage humans have done."

Silas was thoughtful. "Yes, I suppose they are right. What if we cannot reverse the cycles of Earth to its old rhythm? What if we don't understand what they tell us?"

Helga laughed. "We could understand through our thoughts I suppose. I have been told that there is more than one kind of Orb, but they are all of one race and belong to the Confederation. They could be construed as being neutral, for they do not hold or have any feelings about the information anyone seeks, but have to go off to get it. They cannot predict future events."

Silas laughed nervously, uncertain of his ground. He knew nothing about Orbs and secretly thought it was all nonsense, but he said, "If you think it will help, then go ahead. I for one will get the address of where Kate and Adam are staying. It should not be too difficult. We need to place bugs and hidden recording equipment there. Something we *can* rely on."

CHAPTER SIX

THE GOLDEN ONE ARRIVES

Oh how the stars of the night shine.
Oh what messages they could bring.
Just lose yourself in their time
what you learn could make you sing.

The wisdom of the Creation,
insight into the Mind.
All is there in its fashion,
the origins of Mankind.

You are but little children
stumbling in the night.
All you need do is look upwards
to see the Shining Light.

Many hands are stretched out to guide you,
you have to take but one
to walk safely through the darkness
and be at last with the Son.

The Mothership, now re-positioned into a deep crater on the far side of the Moon, buzzed with anticipation and excitement. The Golden One, from his status far above that of the Galactic Confederation was making a surprise visit. Master M was overseeing all welcoming arrangements. He called in his two trusted Time Travellers, Sechem and Jamère. Their other duties would have to wait until the visit was over, and he hoped that his granddaughter Kate and her father would be safe without them. Their safety now rested with Adam, even though his abilities were limited. Although he too was a Time Traveller, he was now an incarnated human being.

The big conference was soon to start and there was much to do. In keeping with Mothership rules, which act as a neutral zone, all were expected to attend irrespective of their stance on the survival of the Human Race. This meeting was to be a vital and unusual occurrence, not only in the Solar System but in the numerous galaxies within the Milky Way.

Jamère jumped up and down in joyful anticipation. “How many humans will be present?”

Master M smiled indulgently. “Do you mean humans on Earth or elsewhere Jamère? You will have to be more specific in your questions if you want answers. Many on Earth would do well to remember that when they ask questions of the spirit world.”

Sechem couldn’t keep quiet. “The very words *spirit world* is very misleading, don’t you think? It is all spirit whether inhabiting a physical form or not. Everything is spirit or energy in a variety of forms, or on various dimensions.”

Master M sighed. “What Jamère meant to ask is how many humanoids will be here. To answer, there will be incarnated humans from Earth as well as from other planetary systems.”

Sechem jumped up. “Incarnated humans? You mean alive now?”

“Yes, why not? If they are able to connect and travel through meditation or sleep, why not? Their time here will be limited of course. Your charge Kate has done that many times. Don’t you remember?”

“So, she could come here for the event,” Sechem asked.

"I'll have to think about that," Master M replied. "It would solve the problem of keeping her safe for a while. But for the moment I need to prepare for The Golden One. Remember he is the one who saved us all from Gork."

The two Time Travellers shuddered at the memory of how they were frozen solid by Gork and only the intervention of The Golden One saved them.

"Will Gork be attending?" asked Sechem. "As it is a neutral base, the Mothership and its events are open to all, well intended or otherwise."

"I have no word on that at present. As far as I am aware, he is still contained after breaking the rules of the Galactic Confederation. He may be barred permanently, especially as he now has Valdek to replace him."

A chill crept over Jamère. "I hear that Valdek is worse than Gork. I didn't think anyone could be worse than that awful creature."

Master M frowned and looked worried. He stood up, a signal to the two Time Travellers that the session was over. "I have decided that I will arrange for Kate and Adam to be here. It will be good for them to meet and see Valdek while they are under the protection of the Mothership's rules. It is better to be prepared, eh? Now I must get on."

The two Time Travellers left. They had plenty to think about.

***

That night Adam's house seemed unnaturally quiet. The bushes in the back garden were stilled in the hush that pervaded the property. Not a leaf moved. Jacob's senses were on high alert and Kate felt jittery. Only Adam did not sense anything and hummed happily as he moved around the house. It was a quiet neighbourhood, but they all jumped when they heard the loud screech of an owl as it flew overhead.

"Something is up," said Kate, quietly as if she did not want to provoke whatever might be around.

"I agree," Jacob whispered. "Don't you feel it Adam?

"You both know I am not as psychic as you two. I depend on you more than you can know. Maybe my dealings with the Shadow Government and the people I meet have dulled my senses more than I realised."

Kate sighed. She knew how important it was to maintain regular contact with her cosmic family, but it worried her that she had not been given a mission for quite some time.

"Let's all get a good night's sleep and perhaps we will feel better in the morning."

Kate soon drifted off to sleep, one arm draped over Adam's shoulder, as if she was afraid to lose touch with him. It was the screech of the owl that alerted her that something had changed. Opening her eyes she saw she was standing alongside Adam, both clothed in tight silver suits.

"Oh, we're here again at last," she breathed in delight. She recognised Master M's sacred apartment. At that moment Master M walked into his sanctuary to join them.

He held out his arms. "Come my children. You have special permission to be present at a meeting of the Galactic Lords, called together by The Golden One." Waving them forward they left his room and entered a corridor leading to an auditorium of immense size. Waving bands of light flickered erratically throughout the entire area. Kate watched, fascinated as colours played in constantly moving patterns around the walls. She wondered if the walls were solid as they seemed to be ebbing and flowing in the glorious light display in front of her.

The coloured lights thinned till Kate could see through it. She saw a mass of beings filling the room. In the centre was a huge Pinecone crystal on a raised plinth covered in a rich blue cloth.

Looking around she recognised the blue Birdmen of her childhood who kept her company when she was locked in the cupboard under the stairs by her mother Francine.

She listened as Master M explained who each being was: Grays, small and large, Blond Nordics, Syrians, the Aldabarens, the Anaka, the Annunnaki, the Rall, the Mantis group, the Lion tribe and races from star systems such as Lyra, Vega, Pleiades, Sirius, Procyon, Tau Ceti, Ummo, Andromeda and Arcturus. It was like a lesson in astronomy and she marvelled at this glimpse of the diversity of the universe.

On one side sat a line of what were clearly humanoid beings, some of which had heavy, dull and unpleasant energies emanating from them. This was in complete contrast to another humanoid group standing closer to the Pinecone. This group glowed so brightly it was almost impossible to define their forms. Kate blinked and rubbed her eyes. Was this real or just a dream?

Master M said in her mind, "You are truly here my child. The glowing ones represent the Lords of The Universe, The Galactic Command Council and the Planetary Programme for the Grand Spiritual Experiment."

The walls and all seating ebbed and flowed in so many colours and reminded her that she was not consistently in one dimension or the other. She was fluctuating between the various levels. But this was a level she hadn't experienced before in all her earlier visits. She looked round at Adam.

Feeling a light touch on her arm she moved forward with him as Master M guided them to their seats. A stillness fell over the enormous collection of beings from all over the Universe. The Golden One was about to enter. To her delight and astonishment divine music filled her ears such as she had never heard before. She tried to collect her wits and clutched Adam's hand tightly.

"Do you hear that Adam?" she whispered.

"Shush," he said. "he is coming."

From the entrance a stream of glorious angels came in, slowly and majestically followed by a figure of such brilliance of golden light that it dazzled their eyes. Master M moved forward to greet the magnificent figure and guided him to a seat. A reverent hush fell over all present.

The Golden One rose to his feet. "I have called this unusual meeting to discuss once more the Planetary Programme for the Grand Spiritual Experiment on the planet Earth and to see how it is progressing. So many times we have sent Masters, whole groups of highly evolved souls to incarnate as babes or to take on human form in order to swing the balance between good and evil. You may remember Simeon Toko, Sai Baba, Jesus, Moses and so many others too numerous to name. Then there were the Avatars such as Buddha and Krishna. I ask you all now as members of the Galactic Confederation if you have noticed any difference in the behaviour of the Human Race as a result of their presence on Earth?"

At first there was a deathly hush and reticence to speak, then suddenly the Great Hall erupted in a riot of voices. Master M raised his hand to silence them. "One spokesman at a time please." He pointed his long arm to one group making the most noise.

"They are in the shadow" Kate muttered to Adam. "I can't see them clearly at all. I have a bad feeling about them," she added.

"That is because they do not have a spiritual light in them, and I wonder if they have souls at all" Adam grimaced at the idea of beings without souls. He had heard of some races in the universe constructing forms according to what they felt were useful. They had intelligence and minds that created, but were without the silver cord attachment to The Divine Creator. When their constructed forms decay, they are finished forever. There is no chance of continuing through re-incarnation or through a soul journey to reunite with Source. Some of the earlier forms are beginning to rot because of continued exposure to physical dimensions and conditions of a constructed container.

"But how is it that they are allowed at this meeting?" Kate asked.

"This is a Mothership, a neutral place for cosmic travellers. No limits you see."

Kate did not see. "So as long as visitors have joined the Confederation they can come to this meeting? Is that right?"

Adam grunted. "If they obey the rules, yes they can."

Master M addressed the group in shadow. "You first, Valdek." Kate and Adam gasped as the creature seemed to rear up like a wild animal as he got to his feet. Although cloaked in a red flowing gown, Kate could see the physical bulk beneath it. Was this a creature from hell? Tendrils of terror curled in her stomach. Surely a creature such as this could not have been allowed at the meeting, but then she remembered they were on a neutral station and all had the right to speak. Valdek opened his mouth and she saw his tongue flick out like a venomous snake.

"Did you see that, Adam?"

"Scary, isn't he my darling? But he can't hurt us here in the presence of The Golden One."

Valdek began to speak. "With deference, O Great One I think we have waited far too long for the Human Race to change. *We* are still in charge in many places of power on Earth, such as within Elite Powers in Control, and they still have no idea, or better than that, they don't seem to care one way or the other. The general public do not want to be disturbed with profound or troubling thoughts. They do not want their daily routine disrupted. They don't care to awaken - - -." Valdek suddenly stopped mid-sentence as he noticed their little group. He raised a dark scaly arm and pointed it at Kate and Adam. A sudden outburst of rage came from him as he shouted,

"What are *they* doing here? Who allowed it?"

Kate shrank back against Adam, feeling fear for the first time.

Master M thumped his fist hard down on the table before him.

"That is enough, Valdek. You are overstepping the boundaries of your right to speak. It is none of your business who is invited to this neutral ship. Hold your tongue."

Valdek visibly quivered, like a reptile about to strike. Clearly angry, he shouted, "I have been tasked by Gork to find that woman and destroy her. Since you have constrained him he had no choice but to engage me to carry out his work. I have a right to do so in his name."

The Golden One rose from his seat and all present became silent. His words would be listened to above all others. "Valdek, you were asked about your opinion of the Human Race. You have deviated from the question in pursuit of your own interests. *BE SILENT*." It was a command.

Valdek sat at once, grumbling all the while.

Kate held Adam's hand even more tightly. "So we are not free from Gork after all," she whispered.

Master M pointed to another group sitting across the hall, indicating permission to speak.

"Speak up," he said. "providing you have some opinion or insight into the experiment and progress of the Human People, or of closing the programme altogether.

An extremely tall figure, glowing with a beautiful blue aura, rose majestically to his feet. He smiled so gently that Kate struggled to not weep at the love that flowed from him.

"He is a Great One," she whispered to Adam.

"As you know our own race is closely involved in assisting those on Earth to awaken and rise from their slumber," the blue figure said quietly.

"How is their progress?" asked Master M.

At once the tall figure in blue fastened his gaze on Kate. "Sir, that human is one of those we sent to assist us in our purpose. To answer your question we feel positive about the outcome of the Human Race. There are great souls down on Earth doing amazing work, on a group basis or as individuals, for no gain except for satisfaction in knowing that they make a difference. For example, holding charity runs, raising money for research, standing up against injustice, generous actions or donations to aid the poor, the sick or those who need help, and being kind. This is not all, for much action is taken to ensure the survival of endangered species and habitats. We have all witnessed amazing acts of compassion, endurance and courage by caring humans. Many lose their lives so that others can live. What greater sacrifice could any soul give? I could go on, but the list is endless. They do this, not realising that their acts will make them great souls on their journeys ahead. No single act goes unrewarded. Their work done on Earth is raising the consciousness leading to Mass Awakening. Their world will never again be the same, for love has transformed it."

There was a quiet applause as he sat, having finished what he had to say.

"Thank you for your report." Master M bowed to the speaker.

Kate watched in admiration at how her grandfather controlled the meeting.

"May we have your opinion?" Master M pointed to a larger mixed group gathered in a huddle on the far side of the hall. "I understand that you are still undecided."

What appeared to be a silvery looking female surrounded by an orange glow rose to address the gathering, encouraged by her companions.

"She is from Lyra," said Adam. "She prefers to stay in the background as a rule.

When she began speaking the sound from her was like a soft waterfall, gentle, refreshing and one that introduced calm over the listeners.

"I could listen to her voice for ever," Kate murmured.

"From what we have observed humans are doing very well in spite of attempts to disrupt them in their endeavours by others with dark intentions." She paused as she looked over at Valdek. "Humans do not need our help to progress as long as they have the drive to be kind to each other, as most do."

She paused again, seeming to reflect on what to say next, or whether she should say what she wanted to. She continued. "We do not have much interest in what humans do, but since their actions, whatever they may be, affect all of us in the Universe we need to keep a watch on how they are and whether they might progress or downgrade. In our opinion we see that humans frequently look to others to solve their problems for them when they should sort them out for themselves.

"You know well, my Lords of All, that interdimensional races who are self -constructed and who occasionally take on physical forms are incapable of advancing to the Creator Source. They do not have the Silver Cord that connects human souls to Divinity. When their constructed forms decay it is the end for them. They cease to be for they have no soul. However they can do incalculable damage while they exist, even for a limited period. Some of these constructed creatures are present on planet Earth and this should be taken into account." In saying this she looked directly at Valdek.

"Some of this is exactly what you said earlier, Adam," Kate said. She saw the slight ripple of polite applause from those sitting and felt heartened. Maybe creatures such as Gork and Valdek could be defeated and she felt this to be true if the Golden One had a say in it.

The Golden One gave a slight nod in appreciation of the words from Lyra. She sat down and seemed satisfied.

Another from a far table stood to speak. The figure was cloaked in dazzling purple and the shape was unclear due to the brilliance of the colour. Kate watched in awe but did not hear a sound, even though he was obviously communicating, and all present received what was being imparted. Suddenly a great voice in her head said in clear English,

"As you well know, O Golden One that we, the Anunnaki have been around and interacting with Earth longer than humans were there. We are, and always have been, The Federation of the Galaxy and of the Confederation of this Universe. Know that humans are our children and we take a fatherly interest in them. When humans developed further, we endeavoured to guide and assist whenever it was deemed beneficial to their advancement. We tried not to show our form for humans had learnt to fear or destroy anything they did not recognise or understand, and still do, even today. This is particularly true in some parts of their world. Fear seems to predominate. In order to overcome this we introduced into the Human Genome many different genes from many different non-human races. We too can take human form, if and when it is considered to be of service. Please note we do not construct the forms as has been mentioned, but enter through the normal incarnation process. This is the reason why current humans are able to contact and interact with so many advanced species if they desire and apply themselves sufficiently. We will never appear in our own form. We tell you now that many of us are residing as humans on the Earth at this time and are attempting to balance the energies of good and not so good."

From the far side of the hall Valdek could be heard shouting. "Answer the question put to you. Stop prattling on about your own history."

A ripple of disapproval ran through the gathering. Kate instinctively recognised that the Anunnaki speaker was an honoured guest, not one to be reprimanded.

Calls of "Be quiet," rang out.

The great voice resumed in Kate's head. *"As I was saying, current humans have such a mixture of genes in their soul forms that they cannot and should not be allowed to disappear. Not to put too fine a point on it, they may be the salvation of all those races of which they are a part. They have enabled the various races to have the Silver Cord connection to the Great Divine Spirit and as such may continue to exist. So, Valdek, it is vital that the Human Race continues in its journey to progress in an upgrade or even downgrade. So many non-Human constructed Races are degenerating that humans may be their only salvation."*

Kate wondered if this was the reason for abductions and collections of humans by other races. She needed to talk to her father about this later. Now was not the time. She tried to focus her eyes on the surroundings, but everything was becoming blurred. She felt dizzy as she tried to concentrate. The next thing she knew she was waking from a deep sleep. Was it all a dream after all?

CHAPTER SEVEN

JACOB'S JOURNEYS

No use thinking of the past for it has gone, don't think of the future because it has to come, think of the present because that is where you are. *Kazi Shams*

Jacob felt restless. His daughter was so caught up in Adam, and last night she went off with him and he didn't know how to find her. He was worried. Was he losing her? Was she going away from him? As the thought entered his head she walked in with a happy grin on her face.

"Where were you last night?" he asked. "I couldn't find you anywhere. I was worried sick that something had happened to you."

"Oh Dad. We had such a marvellous experience and I still don't know if it was real or not."

Relieved he looked at her happy face, smiled at her and said "Kate, tell me all about it."

For the next hour she related all she could to her dear father. When she finished he sighed.

"I am unable to follow you my darling girl. I am both pleased and sad. What good am I to you now?"

"Please don't be sad. You are needed so much when I go on my journeys. You must know that. I love you and would be lost without you. Don't forget too that we have the wedding to prepare and I need you to walk me down the aisle."

Jacob smiled at the thought, feeling better. Should he tell her what he had discovered? He decided he would.

"Kate, I have some information that might help you understand how important the work is that you do. I too have had my experiences that I have not shared with you so far. I had a voice last night. It was very clear, very loud, and very certain, saying that we are all truly loved by God, and that our lives are deeply important to the existence of the Universe. Our love somehow expands the Universe and does some very important things. I felt that there was something at stake, that we have a very important job to do."

"Oh, Dad how wonderful. It says the Human Race is important and should continue."

"Yes indeed it should. But there is more. Last night I was taken to a large hall where I saw a crowd of people, but they didn't have human form. I recognized them simply as souls. Our job on Earth is important. If we don't learn how to love, there will be very serious, negative consequences in the Multiverse. I had a strong sense that we are needed, and our worth is connected to how much we can love. My belief is that there are multiple dimensions. I have always had a deep quest for knowledge, but that need has now grown much more intense. There was also a presence of non -Earthly beings in that place. You already know this my darling, but what they want is for us to share with others that true reality consists of far more than the small dimensions we have on Earth. We have our five senses on Earth, and it is upon this that we build our entire sense of what we are and who we are and what we are doing here. I know we are deeply loved. The love we have inside us is beautiful and brilliant and is needed on this Earth."

Tears ran down Kate's face as she listened to her father telling her what had happed to him.

"Darling Dad, you are so wonderful and so loved. How could you ever doubt that you are needed?"

"But I have more my darling. I too have my messages in meditation. Can I share this with you?"

"Oh, please do, Dad."

Jacob closed his eyes and took a deep breath before relating his journey as if it were happening as he spoke. "I am wrapped in green and steps take me deeper. I count the steps as I go. The stairs are like green turf, looked after and comfortable to the feet. Trees are on either side and I am reminded of trees that are on a path to a church and cemeteries such as in Italy. At the end of this path is beautiful Eastern temple, someone takes care of this. Clearly, I have to go in.

I ask. "Show me what I have to understand. Show me. "

There are lots of doors going in different directions. I feel that whichever one I take it is going to lead me into the past. There are rooms leading off the path. As I look into each room as I pass there is a person inside. They pop their head round as if to say *hello are you coming in*? But I don't feel yet that I have the right one.

"It stretches back in time, is the message. All the knowledge that has been gained here comes from the past, the past when everything was known. It has always been known. To discover what is here you need to discover the past."

"I can't understand that."

"Time is irrelevant, but we use the word past for your benefit. In fact it still exists in the present. Think with the mind that is ancient. Don't think with your current mind. Think as if you were already there in the halls of knowledge with the great philosophers, the great mathematicians, all on hand to reveal the secrets of the Universe. They are all there. You just need to decide which one to delve into."

"I'm not sure where to go with this. So many choices and if it is well known in the past it will be in the books, won't it? So I won't be learning anything new."

"You are forgetting where Human beings come from. You are forgetting they came from much further back than that, further than books. For answers to your questions look to knowledge way back in time, way back before the current Human Race."

I ask. "Can you do this now? I want you to do this now."

As I ask, that an extremely tall, fully robed man steps forward. He appears to be ancient, but he is not. He has kind, gentle eyes. He puts his hands out to me. I reach forward and take them, and as I do a current runs through me, heat passes through from him to me. I love it.

"It is a uniting of the mind. A passing of one time to another."

"Wow! That was quite an experience Dad. How do you feel about it?" Kate looked at her father with new eyes. It was a wonderful thing to see. He was joining her in more ways than one. She leant over and hugged him with all her might.

Jacob blushed and looked pleased and embarrassed. "Shall we have some tea?" he asked.

***

Adam was busy in his office in Washington DC. He had been away too many times to avoid his absence being noticed. Even though he now felt that the old General was well disposed towards him he did not want to push his luck. He helped himself to another coffee. He needed to think.

A sound of buzzing caused him to look for the cause. The buzzing got louder until his ears hurt. He searched under his desk, it had to be coming from somewhere. Then he felt a poke on his rump causing him to jump up and hit his head.

"Can't you see me Adam?" it was Jamère up to his tricks again. Adam looked and looked and eventually was able to see him clearly.

"Oh dear, you are losing your abilities my dear friend. This won't do."

"Why can't you arrive like everybody else?" grumbled Adam.

"What is bothering you my friend? We can all feel it from elsewhere."

"How can you help?" Adam sighed. "Kate and I are to be married."

"Oh, my word, you are not having second thoughts, are you?"

Adam gave a big sigh. "It is just that she loves me for my body and what she sees. I'd like her to see my soul, for this body is not mine, it's one I have taken. The soul though, it might be shining or not so bright. I am not the body. If she could only realise that the body that I have taken through this borrowed incarnation is a composite of the genes of his parents, the environment in which he lived, and the experiences lived during incarnation. If she could see my own soul, irrespective of the garment I have put on. If only she could see the soul within my body."

Jamère laughed loudly. "Oh you fool. She would love you if you were the ugliest creature on Earth. It *is* your soul she loves. Do you think Master M would allow his own granddaughter to marry the wrong person? You are a fool."

Adam breathed again. He smiled, but at the same time he worried about losing his psychic abilities. Was being in a human body causing this?

Jamère looked at him in concern. "I'll tell you what we will do, if you are game." He waited.

Adam said, "Whatever it takes. Let's go for it."

"If you are sure, I will let you experience a prediction given by the Angelic Force. What you do with it is up to you. If your psychic senses are too dulled, you will not receive anything. Do I have your permission?"

"Yes, yes. Stop messing about."

Adam settled down in his chair, closed his eyes and allowed himself to go into a deep place. Jamère watched him carefully as he said.

"The Angelic Force is coming in saying about Earth Changes to come."

Soon Adam heard a voice in his head.

"The Earth is one cell of a giant body, a giant everything. Cells can divide. I give you a picture of the Earth splitting into two, in the way a cell divides. I give the word 'cloning'.

Adam did not understand.

"We will explain this, rather differently if we can, for purposes of illustration. As to the future, the Angelic Force and those who would protect, oversee and guide evolution of the Creation, not simply the planet Earth but all of Creation. The Force and the guidance that this is able to produce, that can appear, can indeed materialise a completely new cosmic body, in form relative to the Creation concept. It can seem miraculous and relatively instantaneous. However, if you think in terms of time, then this is protracted. We do not think in Earth time and we know, for it has been decided, that a new cosmic body can be produced for the benefit of the souls of humankind. So indeed, in your words, it could be called a cloning."

Adam: "Has this been done before?"

"It has. You might call yourselves experimental. You might even call yourselves a prototype, for we are modifying, improving and producing yet better models as time goes on. We find it difficult to put into your language. It has been done before, and no doubt it will be done again in the future."

Adam asks again: "Souls who take part in this experiment, do they agree to do this?"

"They agree as they progress. There isn't agreement in total, by all souls at the same time. As their own lives renew, or die, if they are physical then they are faced with choices. The choices are put before them and they may agree, or they may not. Each soul will progress according to its choice. So, yes, there is agreement for those who wish to follow the Earth's progression. Nobody is forced into anything. Gravity will reassert itself."

Jamère was concerned when he saw Adam slumped in his chair and looked as if he might fall off. He shook Adam hard as he appeared to be losing his energy field. Had he taken him too far?

"Adam come back to me," he called. Adam stirred, opened his eyes and looked at Jamère with a huge grin.

"Wow! Is that what it is like for Kate when she goes down?"

Jamère laughed, relieved. "Not exactly but close enough. "Now do you understand why she will not stop?" He now realised he had two charges. Kate and Adam.

***

All was not quiet in another part of DC. Silas and Helga moved round and round each other like gladiators preparing for a fight.

"Silas, you have done nothing but suck up to that awful creature Valdek and where has that got us? Nowhere. Kate is still poking her nose into affairs that do not concern her. We have her energy signature, but have not acted in bringing her in. Why? What are we waiting for?"

Silas grunted. "We do not have enough to prove she is invading our secret bases. We do not have hard evidence."

"When has that ever stopped us before? We could easily arrange an accident and get rid of her for ever." Helga stamped her foot in frustration.

"But Valdek told me that she is for him alone to deal with. My hands are tied. He has plans of his own for her. And don't forget Gork. He may be constrained, but his mind is still active, and he is working hard on getting her. He has a personal agenda, I am sure of it."

Helga thought hard. "You are a fool Silas. If anything happened to her, he couldn't prove we had anything to do with it. Accidents do happen every day. Leave it with me."

CHAPTER EIGHT

TEAM WORK

Whenever you meet new opportunities,
grasp them with both hands. Don't let them go.
Utilise all the forces for good that dwell within you and direct
them towards these new openings. They will surely flourish
and grow. The effect of this growth will spread outwards.

In Bethesda Kate was restless. Adam was absent more often than before due to keeping up his pretence of working for the Shadow Government. They were still waiting for documents and visas, and preparations for the wedding were on hold. What was going on in England? It seemed so long ago when they were there – it was another world. What was happening with Poppy and her mother? What were they thinking? Perhaps if she meditated with the intention of connecting, it would give her some answers.

She called her father. "Dad, now that you are having your own journeys so clearly, do you think you could help with one for me?"

Jacob got up from his seat by the window where he had been reading. "Always ready, my darling. Shall we do it now? There is not much going on and I am getting bored. Usual method?"

Together they prepared the room, drew the curtains, turned off the phones and settled to wait, as Kate took herself down. She began to fade from Jacob's sight but encouraged by his own experience he felt able to deal with whatever might be presented. She would be alright, even without Sechem and Jamère.

"Speak to me Kate. I need to hear you," Jacob called.

In a quiet voice she began.

"The stairs are very narrow, going down into a cellar, or so it seems. It winds down. As I get to the bottom it widens out, opening into something. It has a gritty floor, not sand, the kind of grit that forms on concrete. As I move forward, there's an echo to my footsteps which is a bit odd. This place is quite large, like a cave. But this is not a normal natural cave as on a beach. It is inside a mountain.

A hand reaches out from somewhere, a strong hand grabs me and pulls me into a nook, a cranny that I would have passed by had the hand not dragged me into it. It's a narrow side passage that leads to something much bigger. I already know that in advance, as if my mind is ahead of what it expects. All I can feel is the force of the hand pushing me forward into a very large space, still inside the mountain. It is very manmade, very set with regular proportions, there's not much finery about this. It is bare. I walk forward and whoever is pulling me along, I can't see, but I can feel. They are invisible to me.

"I keep being guided. There is machinery, not that I would recognise what the machinery is for, it is quite large. We walk past that. This whole area is the nuts and bolts of whatever is ahead. To ensure smooth running of what's ahead.

"I'm totally trusting I walk forward, not seeing far ahead. The passage is now well lit, colour coded I'd say. The colours are direction links. I feel I've seen this before. You need to know which colour leads to where. The colour is on the floor, so I just follow the colour our that I am being brought into. It's an odd orange brown. It would be difficult to see it if you weren't looking. There are others leading off the path. It's quite a long journey, this one.

"Show me what I need to see please. Why am I here?"

"We enter into a more refined place. There's seating, desks, computers, all clearly indicating connections with the airwaves. There are screens. I'm guided through the desks to an office."

"Wait outside." A voice tells me.

"I sit on a seat for a while. A door opens. That is interesting; a person in jump suit comes out. It's a female in a tight-fitting outfit. For some reason I'd expected a male. I can't see what country she represents. She is very much like any other human being and isn't an alien. She invites me in, to what I can only assume is her office. She has a lot of instruments in front of her on her desk."

"What am I supposed to do?"

"You are now one of us. You have been enlisted as one of us."

I repeat: "Enlisted? What am I supposed to do? What does this mean? What am I supposed to do?"

"We want you to use your psychic abilities to gain information and report back."

"I need to know, is this a 'set up' for the benefit of the planet Earth, or for unwelcome beings from space?"

"This is to protect and ensure the survival of those who can run this planet on a more spiritual level later on, when it is for the betterment of all the people who remain."

"This seems to indicate that not everybody will remain."

"You already know this is true."

"What about the stories I've heard, that those who control the planet for their own nefarious interests have built tunnels? Some of them go as deep as 42 levels."

"That too is true. These are being dealt with as we speak. They have been used in the most diabolical way that cannot be tolerated. You may hear loud booms and strange noises across the land and be puzzled. What you hear are the tunnels being cleared, and when this is done, we dynamite them so that they will never be used in the same way again. These are the noises you hear.

"But we too have *our* tunnels and *our* operational set-up to ensure survival of those who will benefit the planet? They are conducted by your military, alongside those who wish you to survive. You are now in one of *our* tunnels."

"So, this indicates there will be a war between the two factions again."

"There has always been war between two or more factions. This is unlikely to stop."

"So, are you receiving help from our Cosmic Cousins?"

"We work together as always. This is where you are needed, for you can communicate more easily than we can. We can obtain their help through you."

"Is what you are giving me now for pure information, a warning, or is this as it is going to be?"

"It is all these things. You are playing a part, as you well know. At the same time you are bringing into reality what is required for all Human Races."

"What about the planet Earth itself?"

"Are you ready for another view?"

"Yes of course. I must get as much as I can."

"Are you ready?"

Without waiting for my answer I see a big television set, but it is a panoramic view, like a viewing point, like a television screen without a boundary. All I can see is a sea with a big rolling swell on it. I can feel the motion. I can see underneath the sea as well. Under the sea are mountains; I can see mountains below the water. As I watch the water is stilled, frozen, a dead stillness.

A guide sitting with me and watching says: "Everybody thinks of the warming as being a raising of temperature. Consequences are not always as expected; the consequences of altering cyclic weather patterns to such an extent is that in certain areas there is a dramatic lowering of temperature not previously imagined.

A shift in position of temperate zones. Siberia one imagines as being the area of intense cold. That is a mistake; there will be a reversal. Those now wishing to be anywhere but in Siberia will gladly remain there. A land of plenty, of abundance, of pleasurable existence."

He shows me a land peopled by many; they are short people, very short. I see vast canopies, enormous expanse of covering by manmade artificial material over the land. I don't know if this is here or on another planet.

"It is a means of existence elsewhere, perfectly practical and feasible. One that may need to be created for the continuance of life in certain areas."

"Talk about science fiction!"

"What is fantasy to you is quite normal for those who live in this manner. Your method of existence to the eyes of many, appears to them to be fantasy, a world in the imagination only. We who have communication and knowledge know, and fully realise that there are many facets to life, as you yourselves are aware that thought alone is also an existence. There are many worlds that even you would find difficult to comprehend."

She is showing me squares and triangles and shapes in colours and they are all moving about - everything is a shape of geometric form.

"That too is a reality every bit as valid as your own."

"The Earth will always be safe no matter what the human mind does to it. That need not be your concern at all. Your concern and ours should be about the spiritual journey of the Human Race, the spiritual ongoing journey of the Human Race. You as advocate for a betterment can work with us and the Cosmic Cousins. Have we made this clear?"

"Yes, but why all this business of going through the tunnels? Why couldn't you just bring me here?"

"You know as well as we, that you need your journey down into an altered state to be here. What you call 'Mind Travel', remember. Mind Travel journeys are as real as living and breathing is in your everyday world. We simply bring you into contact with us. It's very simple."

"Can you give me some evidence that what you are saying is valid, is true?"

The woman turns around, opens a door behind her by pressing a button. Out step three extremely tall extra-terrestrials. Two are female and one is male. They are smiling at me and I feel a wave of emotion and love. They are so tall that I feel puny beside them.

"You needn't worry about size. It is inside that matters," says the woman in a jump suit. "Is this proof enough for you?"

"At that I feel I have to come back because my chest is hurting now. Something is going on with me, physically. I feel it. I must stop."

"Kate, Kate," Jacob called out to her as she slumped over in the chair, almost falling off. "Come back to me." This was not what he expected at all, but then he realised that her connections usually had their own agenda. What were they to do with all that information?

A short time later the two of them revived themselves with a strong cup of tea and wished Sechem and Jamère had been present.

***

Jacob encouraged by his own journey, was keen to do more. Perhaps they would give him important information too. He had to find out. What better time than while Adam was so taken up with his other work. He never did like sitting around doing nothing. He broached it to Kate over breakfast. He watched her as she tucked in to a bowl of cereals.

"My darling, do you think you could sit with me if I took another journey?" He watched her reaction and was delighted to see her eyes shine at the prospect. "How about this evening?" he said.

After they had settled, they made their preparations which always included a prayer. They plumped the cushions and drew the curtains. Jacob sat upright and waited for what might be shown to him. Kate listened as he began to speak.

"I am going down a slippery winding path. I am slipping a bit because there's growth on it, like slime, as happens on steps leading into water. I need to be careful how I tread. At least there are rusty railings on either side that I can hold onto. It's very windy and I have to hold on tight, so I don't get blown off. All these things signify that I have to take care. Take care! The path ends in a well-kept area. It has been tended and there are clean sweeps of landscape."

"Show me what I need to see please."

"It's interesting because I'm looking at scenes of ships on Earth, all kinds. Each ship has the word 'Earth' written on its side. Many different kinds of Earth ships are there, not just our own. They are all going in separate directions and all have diverse destinations."

"Each one will experience something dissimilar to the other. Which one will you decide to get on? It's your choice, as each one will have a unique experience."

"What is this telling me?"

"When you set out on a journey to any destination you generally do some research and find out about the destinations and the kind of conditions you might be going to experience. According to your own will you choose one. That is exactly what is happening with the planet Earth right now. The inhabitants of planet Earth must look ahead to possible futures, possible conditions depending on which Earth vessel they choose. Some are good, some are not, some are exciting, some are boring. But it will be the inhabitants of Earth who decide.

"How are they going to be able to see the conditions of the separate Earth's? How are they going to see, because individuals in general do not? They just scoot through their journey. They don't look ahead. They don't think about what they need."

"This is precisely the difficulty the Earth is facing. Each will have a journey and each individual will choose their own future."

"Will they be guided? Will they be assisted in making a decision? Will they receive any help?"

"That is dependent upon the mind of each person. It will depend on whether they have enquiring minds at all, and whether they do any research for themselves., As a result of what they do, their thoughts will lead to making their decision. Do you see?"

"Where do I come into this because nobody will listen to me? Should they listen to me at all?"

"If they are drawn to listen, they will. If not, then what you do will have no effect on them whatsoever."

"Oh, so what I am doing could be a complete waste of time?"

"No second of your existence is a waste of time."

"I do wish I understood more. I really do. I don't feel as if I am getting anywhere here in getting this information."

Kate could feel his frustration since it mirrored her own in many times. At the very least her father could now understand her more through having his own journeys.

"Wake up Dad," she said gently touching him on his arm. "How are you feeling?"

***

Adam was encouraged by his experience with Jamère's help. Could he do it alone he wondered. Back in Bethesda, lying alongside Kate as she slept soundly, his mind went over and over what he had been given. He wanted more, much more, and fell asleep.

Sechem and Jamère watched them as they slept. “It’s working,” they said. “The plan is working. We will get them all working together as Master M intended. He’ll be so pleased. Shall we give Adam a dream? That will help I think.”

A loud snore escaped from Adam, but he did not stir. “Now is the time,” Sechem said, and waved his arm over the sleeping man. I’ll give him someone to talk to while he’s under. How about that?”

Adam sees an old man in his dream and asks, “What am I walking on?”

“Your stairs are leather clad. Old green leather bound in time. The steps you take are also bound in time, and as with old books we too have our means of maintaining records. You are on a journey. Listen, feel as you go. You have taken the journey to times past and future. Smell the leather, it has a particular smell about it.”

“Each step down is taking me deeper into the realms of the past. I’d rather go into the realms of the future and what we are doing for our future.”

“What we have said, you already know.”

“Give me something I don’t know, something I can put out.”

“Keep walking.”

“I am standing in reeds, but not in water.”

“Water has been here before and will come again. There will be a time when the tops of the reeds will be submerged. But for now you and the world can walk through much of the land that later on you will no longer see, for it will have disappeared.”

“What does that mean?”

“It means that much of your world will be inundated and much that you see now will not then be evident to the eyes.”

“How far into the future is this?”

“Not as far as you might think. It is necessary as part of the evolution of the Earth. It has done this before. All have survived, maybe taken a backward step, but all will re-surface as do the souls of man. When they surface anew, it may not be the last time."

"What encouragement can I give since what you are saying seem to be predictions?"

"As always, it is for each individual soul to make a difference. It is not only for those who feel they are in power. Each soul will journey on their own towards their future. Much of what we say you already know. Likeminded souls will group together, as has been done at the very beginning of your journey. You will attract to you and to each other, souls that are in harmony with each other, and with the same purpose of gaining a greater understanding of their existence. You will congregate together as you have always done. Likewise, those who show no interest, or who do not wish to take an active part in their soul journey, they too will congregate, collect together. They too will need to interact with the surroundings that they have created and are still creating. They will remain in their comfort zone. Each will progress according to their soul's desire. You may say that much of what they have created is not enjoyable, but that too is what they have created. That too is what the soul has created so that understanding may eventually take place."

"How can I help through what you are telling me?"

"Once again we tell you that each individual creates what is ahead. Thought process, the desire, the construction of that desire forcibly and repeatedly enough times becomes the reality that it has striven for. Again, we repeat so often, that the mind constructs, it creates.

"Many on your planet wish to return to their star homes, feeling that things will be better if they can return. This may be the case and it may not, for what is the purpose of the soul? Whether it be another planet or whether it is the planet on which you are currently existing, the goal is still the same, to further understanding and experience Divine Intelligence. Each one decides where it may be to their advantage, to be here or there, or to be somewhere quite different for the experience. It is what is gleaned from that experience that is the vital component. Again, it's the desire and the thought processes that directs each soul to its destination, or along its journey to its destination.

"To give you more of an idea of what we are trying to tell you, would you like another possible future?"

"Yes, please, if you think it will help."

"Here is another scene for you. Are you ready Adam? Tell me what you see."

"I can see in my mind's eye an expanse of industry, factories, smoke. It's an industrial scene. As I look there is a great big wave, as high as it can go. It is rolling across as a wave of red, a wall of red that is sweeping across the land. Like pulling a shutter of red across the scene, it is covering everything as it goes. The industrial scene can no longer be clearly viewed through the red anymore. The wave of red, right way across has the quality of infrared, not a solid bright red. Out of the obscurity step Human Beings, in two's at first, holding hands, an older and a younger. As I watch and try to recognise them, other humans are stepping out of the red, silently holding hands, in two's, just stepping out of the gloom. Many are following and stepping out of this that has descended upon them. It is a strange thing to describe and I cannot identify, but just know there are Human Beings stepping forward and surviving what has overtaken them. They are silent, no words, just two by two, not a great horde. Slowly, but with a sense of bewilderment, with a sense of coming out of dreamtime, and not really fully aware of what has happened. Dazed and recovering, but with a sense of bewilderment and shock about them. They have survived.

"What period of time is this.

"It is when your industrialisation has reached the pitch where it cannot be contained any longer. When it reaches explosion point and cannot be encompassed within the law of things. That is when this scene will take place."

"Well, I am focussed at the moment on what's going to happen to the Human Race and to Earth. I need help in that area."

"We have already given you possible futures. Do you wish us to change that future?"

"Yes, some of it, yes."

"Again, we bring you back to the mind. The mind constructs its future, that of yours as well as all the others. It's not so very difficult to understand. If you wish to change what has been predicted, then you must create alternatives. Actions must go along with that creation. Create the future that you wish to enjoy and exist in. For those who wish to return to their original star system, they must focus on that, think about it, research it and have their minds dwelling on it so that they have a greater chance of creating that reality. You have often said that we in our spirit way have set things in motion, that everything is planned. That to some extent is true, but our planning goes along with your soul's desire. Do you see what we are saying?

"We *know* what each soul's desire is. We are not talking about an individual incarnation, we are speaking about the desire of your Higher Self, your overall soul's desire here, the Master Soul if you wish. We *know* what the objective is from *that* position. It may touch a chord in those who are awakened to a higher source of themselves. To those who have no idea, they might wonder why such and such a thing happens to them, why their life is this way or that way. They feel sure they did not create and would not want it. We say to you that at a higher level of your soul that intention was set. It was set before you came into a physical form. It was set often before your incarnation. So yes, it is set, but it is set by you from a very early time. In some incarnations you meet the requirements for yourself and in others you do not. That means coming back and continuing, in order to fulfil your own goals.

"You must find a way to put this in small steps so that it is understandable."

"That's a lot of work."

"But you are capable of it and we know from researching your background from the beginnings of *your* Higher Self, Master soul, the Oversoul as you have named it, the one at the very beginning made its decision as to what it required in order to return to The Source completely. It does go back and there are a lot of steps along the way."

"I don't know if I can do it in this one incarnation."

"You will do what is required for this step of your journey. You have done this before. This is another re-run, for many there are re-runs for souls on your planet. It is simply having another go at what was attempted before. Many attempts were made in the Atlantean period and many times before that.

"We tell you now that there are other aspects of you that are living lives, and that in each you are conducting specific incarnated journeys and non-incarnated journeys in order to fulfil the desire that was set out at the beginning of your Oversoul's journey. It stretches back a long way and will stretch a long way forward. You are in an interim period. All are interacting simultaneously. You are absolutely not alone in your journey.

"Much of the information that seeps through, that you call upon us for, does come from other aspects of your soul. Remember you are connected. We are all connected - *we* are connected with you. You simply need to call on us and have us in your mind."

"I would very much like to psychically see a little more."

"You ask to see the spirit world around you and to be more aware as many other psychics are able to do. We tell you that when a psychic visually sees, by that we mean with physical eyes, not just a mind picture, when you visually see a spirit, the one they see is either from the higher levels of your third dimension or lower levels of the fourth, meaning that they are still very attached to the Earth, for whatever reason, and so the journey to reach you and be seen through those dimensions is not so very great.

"The reason you are not seeing them is that you are aiming for the higher levels of vibration, so high that they cannot be seen. These souls have no need of a body. As we are now communicating with you, and you cannot see us, unless you have a mind construct just to make you feel comfortable.

"We can draw on a memory of what we have been in the past and show that if it is required. Many Masters may do that. There are many psychics who can see and describe and even draw spirit forms which are seen through the mind, not with physical eyes. Otherwise we do not have anything you can see except as an energy form. Even that energy, though unseen, may be simply felt. We don't mean by a sensation of touch but by sensation of the emotions and feelings, the knowing. Do you understand this? Please do not fret that you cannot do what so many do on your planet. Set yourself a goal to reach the highest levels. Each time you meditate you do this.

"We tell you that the very highest levels will never be seen. Even when you pass from this world, depending on your own vibration, they may still not be seen. Any visuals of us are constructions of the mind to make you feel comfortable or connected. They are still valid. You may communicate as you are doing now. This is purely through the mind waves and *our* constructs that enable us to reach through.

"You are already speaking our language on occasion because of the value of sound waves, the value of vibration upon thoughts. That is why we may use sound language. The value of the effect of sound is not often understood sufficiently. Sound is of utmost importance in communication, every sound as a vibration, that while it may not be heard, the effect is there. It is interpreted and understood by those on the receiving end. Continue to speak our language when you feel the urge."

Adam stirred and turned over.

"Look, look," Sechem said. "He is losing the connection. So often any movement of the body breaks the connection with the dream, but I truly think that is more than enough for now."

"Yes, I think so too. Dreams are so important, but often forgotten," Jamère said. They left him sleeping and quietly withdrew.

***

Adam woke early. The sun was streaming in through the window and he felt good, really good. He turned and watched Kate as she slept. He loved her so much. Would she understand his dream? Although only half remembered it had put so many things in perspective for him. He accepted that he was so much more than just a replacement for Colonel Adam Fenshawe that was. He acknowledged that it was his soul that mattered, not the body. He had a role to play in the bigger picture. He got up and left her sleeping.

Outside in the garden he breathed the fresh air deeply and with gratitude for his life. He was at peace. He sighed with pleasure as he contemplated his role. It wasn't so bad being in a physical body after all, in spite of having to be a Trojan Horse within the Shadow Government. He had Master M to thank for that. He heard an owl calling, reminding him it was time to attend to practical matters. Everything would fall into place. Whatever life was going to throw at him, he would cope.

With renewed confidence he decided he would take Kate and Jacob to see the famous Mushroom House as a treat. It was famous because although it started out as anormal regular home the owners decided to extend and modify it to suit a growing family. They covered it in free-flowing, polyurethane foam. And each day, they'd stand back and tell the builders to bring it in here or stretch it a little more there. They never intended for it to look like a mushroom but over time, the name stuck. Adam was almost certain they did not have anything like it in England.

CHAPTER NINE

SURVEILLANCE

Eyes that you do not see are upon you. Every move is noticed. Where your actions are to assist someone else, angels' eyes light up with joy and delight. They know that all is not lost upon the planet Earth and the heart is lightened.

Silas's innards stirred with an excitement he hadn't felt for a long time. He had been given a lifeline in discovering that Kate and Jacob were right there in Washington DC, and best of all, staying at the house of Colonel Adam Fenshawe. This was his chancc, and if he had his way Helga wouldn't be able interfere. His eyes narrowed to slits as he looked at her across the room as she was busy messing with papers in her bag.

"We had better separate," he told her. There was to be no more asking or suggesting he decided. He was in charge, but he couldn't know that Helga had the same notion.

"No," she said. "We'd better stay together. We'll have a better chance if we pool resources. I already have contacts who can give us their address."

"You mean that crazy old coot, the General? The one who lost control of the meeting with Valdek?"

Helga muttered something under her breath but didn't reply. Silas knew he had scored a point. He would do it alone. He left the room. He would go directly to the team and instruct them to trace any energy signal that Kate Greene would leave if she had one of her mind journeys. Dead easy! They would zap her with a HAARP laser the instant she travelled out of the third-dimension vibration. This would destroy her mid travel or freeze her in another time. He chuckled at the thought. Nothing could save her then, and both Gork and Valdek would be delighted with his work. Promotion at last. He would be able to join the team.

Again, he couldn't know that Helga had the same idea. She would be rid of Kate forever. It was late afternoon and the building housing the special surveillance team tasked with locating any energy signal that fell outside permitted and recognised wavebands. Any discovered were immediately reported to another team for authority to act or not. There was sometimes a short delay in response which could be too late or not, depending on the duration of change from one vibrational energy to another. Silas knew this very well and also knew that the team could pinpoint the origin of a signal. Many had experienced sudden inexplicable deaths as a result. It was a good, almost fool proof way of eliminating troublemakers.

Anyone watching might wonder why a smartly dressed man would be in the sort of neighbourhood where the building was located. The street was barely lit, the darkness broken only by a solitary dim light from a post leaning against a brick wall. Peeling red paint covered the door of number seven, and dirty walkways could be seen in all directions with garbage strewn about. At the corner broken appliances had been dumped. All windows had bars on them. Silas kicked aside beer cans as he reached for the number pad fixed to the wood. The numbers were known only to a few, of which Silas was one. He hoped Helga did not have the same privileged knowledge as he punched in the numbers.

The door creaked open and he entered cautiously. At the entrance he had to turn right down a narrow flight of stairs. He made his way carefully, the floorboards creaking as he went. At the bottom he brushed the dust off his suit and walked along a narrow uncarpeted corridor until he was blocked by a metal door. There was yet another security press pad together with an eye scanner. Silas's heart was beating hard with excitement as he made the correct moves. There was a loud click, the door swung open and he was able to enter.

What met his eyes was no ordinary room. As far as he could see the area was filled with monitors, screens, desks and men and women busy at their consoles. All around the walls large panels showed star constellations, some near and some far away. Most interesting to Silas were displays showing various detailed parts of Earth, cities and street maps. Even more surprising to him was what could be seen inside people's homes, businesses, schools, universities, hospitals, and many public offices.

Silas moved along a passage leading off the large room and found many more sections, all seeming to do the same things, following individuals all over the globe. He thought he knew everything, but this was a revelation to him. He had no idea the surveillance network was so vast. Silas reflected that Big Brother was in full swing.

But he was here to do a task. Where should he start? With over seven billion people on the planet – were they all watched? Surely not, and for what reason would they be? What was the purpose?

He stopped his walk along the corridor. Where to next? He had thought it would be simpler than this. He moved forward again and found a door marked in bold red letters,

INTER-DIMENSIONAL ENERGY SIGNATURES.

This had to be it. Again he was faced not only with an eye scan but with facial and voice recognition. Were they monitoring him too? The thought worried him. How long had this been going on and who exactly were responsible for such detailed surveillance?

Was it the team he hoped to join or others beyond the team? The door slid silently to one side. Taking a deep breath he entered.

Scanning the room, a gasp of dismay escaped his lips as soon as he saw her. Helga had forestalled him. Leaning over an operator's shoulder she was pointing to a mass of squiggly lines on the monitor. It seemed to him she knew what she was looking at.

"Hello Helga," he squeaked. "It appears that we had the same notion." He grimaced, and said with as much conviction as he could muster, "With this amazing technology we'll get them both. How about you go after the Colonel and I'll go after Kate?"

"No, Silas. We'll get them together. I'll see that they are finished one way or the other.

Together they both leaned over the operator and gave instructions.

***

Adam's residence buzzed with excitement. "We are going to get married just as soon as it can be arranged, my darling. You will be safe once the papers and formalities are signed."

An anxious look came over Kate's face as he fiddled with the stack of forms before him on his large mahogany desk. She grasped his hand and took the pen from him as he hovered over the papers.

"I know you have clout Adam, but I don't know how even you can get Francine and Poppy over here at such short notice. They don't even know we are out of England. It will be a shock to them. Poppy has never been out of England and has no passport as far as I am aware.

Adam saw the set look on her face and sighed. "They'll understand my darling. They can stay here. There is enough room for everybody."

“I am not getting married without Poppy. Mother can do what she likes, and anyway it could be awkward with her being in the same house as Dad.”

Adam hesitated before broaching the next thing, but he had to do it.

“Remember I told you about the old General? He had been keeping tracks on me and was suspicious of my actions and non-attendance at many meetings. I have been able to put him off and explain my absences were to do with my need to see you my love. He is a romantic old fool at heart and seems to be satisfied with my explanation but needs evidence of my intention.”

What has that got to do with anything?” Kate looked puzzled.

Adam took her hand in his and kissed it. “It would help if we invited him to the wedding, don’t you think?”

Kate smiled. “I like sweet old gentlemen Adam, in spite of his stern face and belonging to the Shadow Government. However, I think it is a good idea. Now let’s get Poppy and Mum over.”

A sudden gust of wind blew the window in Adam’s study open. The papers on his desk scattered across the room. As they both scrambled to gather them up, they heard an owl hoot. Looking up they were startled to see both Jamère and Sechem standing by the window.

“You are forgetting us dear friends. Are we not invited?”

Kate laughed. “Of course you are,” she said. “Have you been listening to our conversation?” Kate tut tutted. “But you can’t be seen, not at any cost. You cannot blow our cover. Do you understand that?”

They bowed low together. “Understand? Of course we understand. But we are here on other matters. We have two jobs for you to do this evening. They cannot wait.”

Delight mixed with dismay crossed her face. She had so much to do before the wedding. Adam was quick to see it. “It will be alright Kate. You know they wouldn’t ask if it wasn’t important.”

"When?" asked Kate.

"Now, immediately," Sechem said. "You remember some time back you encouraged new souls to come to Earth, and told them that if they didn't like what they saw they could change it?"

"That was when we were living in Berkshire, wasn't it? Oh that seems so long ago now."

"No, you have it wrong. You lived in Hampshire, not Berkshire," Sechem corrected.

"Oh, stop messing about. We are losing time. What does it matter where she was?" Jamère said. "She doesn't know where she is half the time." He laughed at his own joke. "Get it? *Half* the time! See?"

Nobody laughed. The colour around Sechem began to glow even more brightly. "Kate, this is important. Remember you said, and I quote parts of what you told them:

"People do not take a stand against tyranny while they can. So many put their heads in the sand and pretend that the terrible things that are happening on their Earth are not happening at all. It is all a conspiracy, or theory meant to create fear, they say. So many feel they have too much to lose if they rock the boat and speak up. - - - - when there's deep suffering there's no crying. There's silence and patient resignation. They go beyond crying."

"Why are you telling me this now?" Kate was puzzled.

There are many thousands of children who are suffering in unimaginable ways and who have been suffering for some time, and the public generally have no idea of this. Some of these children are those you spoke to before, but there are many more. At that earlier time you wept for them and called out for help. We ask you to do this again, and all citizens of Earth to do the same. Again I quote what you said:

"This is a place that's not reached by world aid associations, for this place is hidden and isn't easily reached by the outside."

All those souls who chose to come and endure living as abused children are doing a magnificent job in raising the emotions of the Human Race and are bringing compassion into so many hearts. While they may not stay on Earth very long they are doing an enormous and amazing job in changing the face of the Earth overnight. They are honoured for their sacrifices. What you are most likely looking at are Great Shining Souls who have chosen to live that life so they can grow even higher in their soul advancement. It takes great courage to do that. Many who have easier lives, born into a world where education is taken for granted, where food is abundant and where sickness is attended to would not have the enormous courage needed to volunteer for such an existence."

Sechem reached for her hands and looked into her eyes. "We of the spirit world now beseech you to ask again for the rainbow bridge to reach down to them, and for it to be a bridge for the angels and the light, so that they can travel this bridge when they wish to leave. Ask for something better for them. You're to take them. You're to lead them to the bridge and to encourage them to go over it to the arms of the angels."

Kate saw the earnestness in his voice. Without any further hesitation she sat, set her intention and took herself into a deep meditation. Maybe she could help some of the children. A little time passed before she entered another world. Memories surfaced of when she had helped to release so many imprisoned off-planet beings, so many misnamed 'aliens', who she now knew were her cosmic friends. Soon her vision was filled with lights, all colours of the rainbow. Vague indistinct forms moved about before her. She knew without any doubt that they were angels waiting for the children and that they would take care of them.

Kate did as she was instructed and asked for the rainbow bridge. She watched with awe as the bridge materialised and filled the space with a glorious light. One by one all the suffering children from all over the world moved towards it, stretched out their arms and walked into the rainbow. It was done.

Tears ran unchecked down Kate's cheeks.

Utter silence was in the room as Kate returned to herself. After a short time Sechem applauded, followed by Jamère and Adam.

Jamère was the first to speak. "Good job." He took on a serious look, so unusual for him, and then turning to Kate said, "We have always told you that it has to be the people of the Earth making the changes, not us. However what you did helped those children who had died, or who were going to die as a result of the lives they endured. But there are still so many young ones suffering due to circumstances of birth and at the hands of human beings. Can I ask you to remind people everywhere not to put their heads in the sand and pretend it's not happening?"

Kate and Adam nodded. They would do what they could.

Sechem tapped Jamère on the arm. "Remember to tell them that their off-world friends do in fact, so many times save, not just children, but many others in times of danger. We sometimes call on the assistance of certain humans to work with us when we rescue or save people from certain death during disasters. With their help we are able to gather them up and take them to our ships and return them after the danger has passed. The presence of a human on the ships ensures that they do not panic while this is going on. Then later on they wonder how it was they were not killed by the disaster."

Sechem was getting into his stride now. "and Jamère tell them how many times in situations where someone should have been killed by a runaway lorry and miraculously found themselves unhurt and on the other side of the road. The list of examples of these things goes on and on."

Jamère shook Sechem's hand off his arm. "I think that is enough for them to take in. "Now then, what about the other task?" he reminded him. "We must get on with this before these two lovebirds get carried away by arrangements for their wedding."

At that moment Jacob walked in. "What's going on? Why are Sechem and Jamère here? Have I missed anything?"

Sechem laughed and put his arm around Jacob. "Not more than usual, Jacob. We have a job for Kate."

"What's new?" said Jacob. He sat down and with anxiety etched on his face looked out of the window.

Kate looked at her father. What was he worrying about now? She became aware of Sechem speaking to her, trying to get her attention away from her father.

Kate, "If you don't do this now there is a strong chance that the actions of some Governments will alter and influence parallel worlds. That cannot happen. Just to think of it appals the Spiritual Galactic Council. Not only parallel worlds would be affected but also many cosmic bodies that are still affected and changed by physical elements. That includes your precious planet Earth."

"What exactly do you want me to do?" Kate asked, worry creasing her brow.

"We ask once again for you to de-fuse nuclear devices. Some governments are planning nuclear war in space. They mistakenly think that if they use their nuclear weapons out there it will not affect Earth. How wrong they are."

"I don't think I am strong enough to do what you ask," Kate said.

"We are calling on others such as you to do the same. Don't worry, for the collective effort will or should be enough." Jamère grinned. "I could do it all by myself," he said. "But these things need to be done by citizens of Earth."

"I'll set the room up," Adam said. "Don't forget to set your intention, Kate."

Kate kicked off her shoes and padded around the room on

the soft carpet. Adam knew how to live in comfort, but realised it wasn't Kate's usual environment. Would she be able to relax enough for this big job?

"Curtains drawn, phones off, doors locked?" Jacob asked. He too was worried. Would his darling daughter be successful? Only the next moments would tell.

Kate settle herself on a hard-backed chair, feet planted firmly and after saying a prayer she took herself down, using her self-hypnosis technique.

"We are with you Kate. Speak to us as you go so we'll know you are safe." Adam and Jacob held their breath as they watched her.

"She's going," Sechem said. "Speak to me Kate."

"I'm drifting Sechem. I don't know where I am being taken."

"Remember your intention to destroy nuclear weapons. No, sorry, not destroy but render them ineffective. That way they will do no harm anywhere," added Jamère.

Kate's body jerked. "Oh, I am suddenly in a mine, a salt mine. Is there such a thing, Sechem? All around me are walls of white, quite dazzling to the eye, quite probably due to arc lights all along the passage. I walk along, for this obviously must go somewhere. There are no gantries such as you might expect for sending things into space. I don't understand it."

"Remember your intention Kate," he repeated. "Keep telling your subconscious what you want. It has to comply with your direction."

"Oh my goodness, Sechem. A tall Being in green just stepped out from a side passage. I have never met one like this before, even at the meetings. It is at least 8 feet. It's a Mantis. Oh, my goodness, it is reaching out for my hand. Its touch is brittle but warm."

Kate gasped. "This is not a hologram. It is real. I think it is going to take me to a control centre. I just know it and it is as if it is speaking to me in my head. Somehow, I know what is in its head.

"There is no need to call me 'it' as I am female. I know your mission and we will take you where you can carry it out. No need to fear me, my child."

"I relax and as we move along the passage widens and there are small closed in brown vehicles on rails, large enough for two people. The Mantis folds herself as we get in and operates the controls using push buttons on a dashboard. We move with a quiet swish as white walls flash by. Eventually we slow down to a gradual stop in front of a barrier.

"This is where I leave you child. Your task is important to us inter-dimensionally, but as we are inter-dimensional we cannot do this ourselves. Humans do not realise that we cannot and must not change the physical third dimensional state. We need you to do this for us. Your own future depends on it."

"All of a sudden the Mantis is gone. As she said, she wasn't able to stay long. I am on my own Sechem. Sechem, can you hear me? I don't feel you around anymore."

"Keep your intention firmly in your mind and all will be well," urged Sechem.

"That is all very well for you to say Sechem but there is a buzzing in my head, and it won't go away. It is interfering. I haven't had that before. I am trying to settle my mind. Keep watching me Sechem"

Sechem began to worry. It should be easier than this, and what was the buzzing?

"Feel the barrier wall. There *is* a way in or the Mantis wouldn't have brought you there."

Kate ran her hands over the wall before her. It was unnaturally smooth. There had to be something, some mechanism. Suddenly she heard a click followed by a whirring sound.

"I've found it. A large panel is sliding aside. I don't know what to do now because as I see into the place there are two military men standing just inside. What if they can see me?"

Sechem laughed. "You silly goose. They can't see you or even sense you, for they are not at all psychic. Walk straight through them."

"Oh, thanks, I feel safer now, I think. This place I am in is filled with rows of desks, screens, monitors and instruments. Most desks have people sitting at the them. They don't appear to be military, but who knows. Looking forward and to the right I see another door. I walk over to it and pass through. Inside it is smaller with fewer desks and more instrument panels. I sense this is it. I had expected to see missiles, but now realise that this is the control room where they send them off. A group of uniformed men and high-ranking officers stand ready at the consoles."

"Do it now," urged Sechem.

"Do what?"

"De-activate of course. Do what you've done before Kate."

Kate frowned and focussed her mind to create images of all the instruments and buttons on the consoles shooting out wires, tangled up and setting off sparks of light all over the keyboards. As she did this it was as if someone had set firecrackers off throughout the room. Pandemonium followed.

"You've done it Kate. You can leave now." Sechem glowed with pride.

Back in the room in Bethesda a few moments later Jacob and Adam breathed a sigh of relief as Kate slowly regained form in her chair.

"This calls for a celebration," Adam said. "Then we can get down to planning the wedding. No more interruptions please Sechem or Jamère."

***

Helga woke early. She paced up and down her rented apartment. It was small, but it suited her needs. Maybe she could steal a march on Silas again and get some news before he did. The results were too sensitive to be sent over the usual channels and she knew that only by a personal visit to the surveillance centre would she be allowed to be told anything.

Stepping outside, a heavy rain fell steadily, threatening to drench her as she hailed a cab. Not being too familiar with the area she had hesitated over hiring a car and driving herself. The cab driver frowned as she gave the address.

"Are you sure you want to go there by yourself in the dark?" he asked. Helga gave him such a look that he shut up quickly. "Right, Ma-am. It's your funeral."

After a while they neared the street. "Drop me at the corner," she said.

Rain gushed along the gutters and she had to step over a flow of debris as she got out. Thanking her stars for her umbrella she walked a short distance to building seven, as it was known. She hesitated, nervous now when she noticed a glowing tip from a cigarette in a shady doorway. She quickened her pace, her heart thumping so hard she could hear it in her chest.

Was Kate's energy signature traced or not? She would soon to find out as she descended the narrow stairs to what she now called The Inner Sanctum. At last she reached the closed door with its bold red lettering. Holding her breath in high anticipation she went through the scanning procedures and stepped inside. The door slid silently behind her. For one moment she forgot that she would not be able to leave unless someone inside pressed the release button. Instinctively and irrationally she felt fear.

A dividing screen blocked her view of the operator she had spoken to on her previous visit. As she moved round it, she saw him, and her legs went weak at the knees. The operator with his back to her was standing at the console talking to Silas. Fear turned to anger. Silas had beaten her to it again. She tapped him on the shoulder, less a tap and more a vicious prod. He jumped, startled.

"Oh, you made it here after all. Look at the display. We've got her for sure. This time she won't get away."

"What are you going to do about her? When are you going to eliminate her?"

Silas scowled. "Not so fast. You know full well that we must get a direct authorisation from the team. They may well want to do the job themselves." Silas paused. "They may even want to use them both for their own purposes. They are good at manipulating the human mind, as you yourself know."

Helga's stomach knotted. Yes, she did know all too well. They had taken her at an early stage in her life and as a result was now mind controlled for ever. There was no going back now and no way out.

"Then we had better let them know, and soon."

Not bothering to thank the operator for his work, they turned to leave together. The rain was still coming down in sheets as they hailed a cab.

***

"It is time we had a little talk." Sechem had his serious face on for a change as he faced Kate early one morning. She was busy getting her breakfast after Adam had left for his office in DC. Jacob was still snoring and wouldn't surface for a while.

"Sechem, why do you do this? I thought I had enough on my plate as it is. I don't need serious talks. They usually lead to me doing more work." She laughed, a little nervously.

"I want to introduce you to the concept of Time and Awareness."

"I thought we had covered that subject many times already.

Enough is enough, Sechem."

"This will be different. I promise you. Please sit down."

"Oh, if you must," Kate, intrigued in spite of herself moved into the lounge and sat down. Kate gave a big sigh. "I want to do my usual method of the stairs," she grumbled.

"No need. We are already connected." The colourful figure gave a little swirl, waved his arms over Kate and she immediately fell into a trance. She was in another world.

"Speak to me, Kate in the way you usually do. You are on another journey, one in which you can learn something new. I will direct you. I am with you all the way. Speak to me."

Kate looked around her. "I seem to be standing next to underground rivers. I say 'rivers' because there is more than one here. They are all going in different directions. I have the choice which one to follow. I am wading through water in the dark. I can hear the water swishing as I go along, just as if I was on the surface, not deep down as I am here. There is a ceiling, a cavern like ceiling. Not like a grotto with stalactites and stalagmites, but this is a river underground. Sechem, what is this supposed to tell me? I know that water will always find its own level and will eventually come out to be seen. But this is pure water coming from the bowels of the Earth so I must be deep down."

Kate heard Sechem's voice. "It has not come from rainfall or melted ice. It has come from Inner Earth."

"But, Sechem I am coming into daylight."

"There is light in the Inner Earth."

"I am a little confused here. Underground tunnels and rivers in the Inner Earth finding its way *down* to a level where there is light? This tells me in order for it to be flowing down to its level, as water always does, it is coming from higher up in the Inner Earth. I have to get my head round this one. There is light in the Inner Earth?

"As I walk along I come out to what appears to be similar to the surface, as if I was on the upper Earth with a grassy plain, trees and bushes. Just like Earth on the surface.

"It's a replica," Sechem said.

Kate puzzled. "A replica indicates to me that it is being made, a copy of that on the surface."

"It is the other way around. The replica is the one on the surface. This is the original."

"You're kidding me. You are getting me more confused now. Never mind, show me what I must see." Kate dismissed what he had said, unable to get her head around this new concept.

"I have been telling you many times that everything that's in your mind is a construction of your mind. This too exists in your mind construct. If not now, but at some point, it will remain in your soul memory."

"Memory implies the past. One can't have memory of the future."

"You haven't got it yet, have you? Past, present and future are all one. According to your mind's intention you can join a timeline at any point in your journey."

"So, tell me then, what part of the timeline are we on now? I'll have to think about this."

"This is the past, the present and the future."

"You're not giving me the answer." Kate felt puzzled and frustrated.

"Today is the past, the present and the future. All as one. In the same way as we have given you the river. The river exists as a river no matter how much water flows along it. It is still a river. What flows along, flows from one direction to the other, timeless movement all existing at the same time. Have I got your attention yet?"

"I have to agree, it has."

"So, you are now looking at time itself and you are looking

at existence, existence being the same, past, present and future, all happening at the same moment but evident and dependant on where you put your attention."

"How is it going to help anybody, knowing that?"

"Remember that whatever you do in your conscious moment will continue to exist, always. Nothing is lost. It carries on into what you might call the future. As I showed you earlier, there are many avenues, many rivers flowing in different directions."

"So, we are back here then to Timelines."

"Call them rivers of existence if it helps you understand. Yes, they are Timelines because everything is. Everywhere is related to time, at least in your Universe. Wherever you find your mind is your moment of time. What you do with your moment in time, at whatever level, whatever branch of existence, is set to exist forever. It's never lost."

"How can we improve as we move along? How can the present moment of consciousness improve our existence?"

"However you react, whatever you do with your moment of awareness has an effect on your continued existence. If your moment of awareness is on a past event it will have an effect on your continuation."

"I feel I've known that. Everybody knows that."

"What we are trying to tell you is, being aware that everything you think, do and react to is important for your continued pleasure, your continued advancement. If you react in a negative way that too influences the continuation of your journey. Be in the moment in the best way you can."

Kate waved in and out of consciousness. "It is a lot to take in and understand Sechem. It is enough, thank you."

Kate discovered she had made toast and had a cup of tea before her with no memory of having done so. It was time to wake her father.

***

Jacob answered his daughter's call straight away. He had been awake for hours, or so he thought. Was what happened to him a dream or reality? He had to share with Kate what he was told. She would understand, and in view of his recent experiences maybe he was after all more in touch with the unseen world than ever before.

"It is time you got up Dad. What have you been doing up there?"

"Get me a cup of tea darling and I will tell you."

A little while later they cleared the dishes with Jacob whistling a tune all the time. He could not put off talking about what he had received any longer.

"Kate, something happened last night, and I still don't know if I was dreaming or if it was real. Can I tell you? You won't laugh, will you?"

"Come and sit down here Dad, next to me. Nothing would surprise me anymore."

Jacob cleaned his glasses and then put them aside. "Um! This is how I saw it. First, I saw a blanket of snow over everything, thick snow, not just a scattering. All marks of identification gone, the snow covering all means of knowing where I was.

"I thought, well no problem, for snow will melt at some point. I was told in my head, this will stay for some time and will cover much of your globe. People will lose their way. What we are showing you is a possibility, that people will have to rethink how they will continue to survive in their world. There will be movement of populations, straggling at first by a few who understood a little earlier than the others, who know they must move.

"Then there will be those who begin to get worried, and as a safety precaution they too will move. Then there are those who don't believe that things are ever going to change, that all will go back to normal, but it will not for a considerable period of time.

They will be the last to move, if they manage to move in time.

"The Human Race will survive, but there will be a re-shuffle if you like, as to where they continue their education and how they will continue their lives."

I asked, "Is this soon?"

"It depends on what you mean by soon. For some soon is next week, for others soon is another generation. We cannot answer this for you. It is not the distant future. There will be movement. There is already movement in the planet itself. Different areas are on a drift. There will be a drifting and re-shaping of the tectonic plates and to some degree, of the continents and their positions. That takes time. That might give you some clues as to what we are saying. It is not the end, for by this time there will be a realisation that there are other worlds, that there are other existences. Movement can be off planet as well. This might give you some encouragement."

Kate looked thoughtful. "Dad, that sounds like a prediction to me. How do you feel about it?"

Jacob smiled happily. "To me it indicates I am opening up more and more to information that is in the cosmos. I am waking up to more and more. I have no reason to fear anything, for I know we will continue no matter what happens. I love life, physical or in pure spirit. I exist."

"Darling father, I love you so much," Kate hugged him with all her might. "Let's go for a walk and enjoy nature. Without the snow," she added laughing.

***

That night, Kate too had her dreams and on wakening she remembered Sechem telling her many months before that he often gave her lessons or information through her dreams when she was too busy with life to meditate and receive that way. We do this with many people, he told her. Was this what had happened to her father?

As if talking to Sechem she went over it again. Was it important or should she ignore it? It had to be important, hadn't it?

"I am on a stony path having come off a swing bridge. The path has some big stones as well as small ones. I must watch my steps and where I tread. There is a line of green leafcutter ants crossing the path and it feels as if I am in a jungle. I can hear animals, monkeys, perhaps and other small animals. There are not many people around, but the path is well travelled, or it would have been overgrown. It leads into a wood with tall big trees, as well as thinner ones, growing very tightly close together; so tight that you couldn't walk through them. They are important and it feels that they have been planted there like that rather than growing there naturally. The air has a humid, warm sticky feel, but not wet. It is comfortable and I feel very comfortable here.

"Oh, this is most unexpected. I come to what looks like a base. I call it a base because it is military. Everything is in order and regimented. It is technical rather than an armoury. It is to do with logistics, technology, wiring and so on. There are people here, both male and female. But I can't really call them people but something similar. Tall, skinny, white. They are clothed, some in tight fitting, some loose clothing, depending on the job they are given to do.

"This is a connection with instruments, so that's a puzzle. I am walking through them and I don't know if they can see me or not, but nobody is taking any notice of me. It's as if I am not there. There are lots and lots of instruments with different colours being played over the instruments.

"Various workplaces are extra important here. Experiments are taking place with colour and sound., sound waves you feel rather than anything you can actually hear. They are putting the two together, colour and sound and looking at the effect. It is an experiment to see how we as humans and animals react to the combination. They are not sure yet of the outcome."

I ask, "How long will they wait?"

"It could possibly be years. But they could be surprised, as with all experiments, sometimes things happen earlier than expected. This is the purpose of showing you this so that you are not surprised."

"What do they hope to gain?"

"There are many uses depending on each sound and which colour. You are already aware that colours have an effect on the human body and have varying uses. This is how they will be applied. To calm someone it would need to have a particular combination and will be used. If other activity is needed then a different combination of colour and sound is used. No one combination covers all. A purpose is applied to each combination. This is an experiment remember. We do not give you a purpose for it is for you to discover rather than show what is already known."

Kate woke and for a few minutes felt she was still in the dream, remembering every word. It was getting harder and harder to tell the difference between dreaming and reality. However, it was time to get on with the day.

CHAPTER TEN

SECRET MEETING

Governments, major corporations, banks, universities and other such bodies view the defence of their secrets as a desperate matter of institutional survival, so much so that the state has gone to extraordinary lengths to punish and/or threaten to punish anyone who so much as tiptoes across the informational line.

In a secluded part of the Mothership, Gork raged against his confinement. There seemed to be no escape from the force field imposed on him. His attendants watched and waited nervously knowing their lord would sooner or later find a way out. After all, hadn't he sent Valdek, his next in command to do his work? Valdek still belonged to the great Spiritual Confederation and had connections and access to Shadow Government arrangements made on Earth. That interfering woman Kate would soon be finished and the spirit line to Master M would be cut forever, and even The Golden One could not stop it.

Back in Washington DC another meeting was called. Adam had no way of avoiding it this time. He wondered who would be present as there had been many changes in the last few weeks. He had been so preoccupied with settling Kate and her father in his home that he had not paid as much attention as he should. He must not forget his role of Trojan Horse and of reporting back to Master M.

The boardroom room buzzed with excitement. There was to be a new chairman. He was quite unlike the former one, they were told. The old General was uneasy and fiddled more than was necessary with his moustache. Adam looked around at the collection of people and was surprised to see the red-haired youth there who had previously asked such embarrassing questions. So he was still alive after all. Adam wondered why that could be and who he might really be. There was so much secrecy around all activities that he dared not ask.

As before, each person attending had a bulky file placed before them which they were expected to read. Adam knew many did not bother and were ignorant of what was really happening under their noses. While they waited for the new chairman to appear Adam opened his folder and began to read.

It was headed: **WE HAVE OPPOSITION TO OUR PLANS ARE THEY RECEIVING HELP?**

NOTES TO THE PUBLIC

July 23rd 2012 3 CME's (Coronal Mass Ejections) in a row headed for Earth passing between Earth and the Moon, but friendly ET's intervened and blocked them from hitting Earth. If they had hit, humans would be toast. More evidence that they wish the Human Race to continue. The USA government also knew of the possible collision and had made arrangements. The Federal Government had an open house picnic for Congress and all its families at Mt Weatherley, which is where they have deep tunnels with huge facilities for Government people. It didn't matter that the rest of the people would die. Interestingly if the CME's had hit, the time it would take for all to perish would have been short.

Colonel Ross Dedrickson, a high ranking military man who spent a long service with the Energy Commission between 1950-1958, claimed that the problems with Apollo 13 were handled with care by extra-terrestrials. A testimony from Colonel Ross Dedrickson, as well as in his obituary, states:

He was assigned to the US Atomic Energy Commission. A long service with the Energy Commission between 1950-1958 included, contract administration duties at Nevada test sites, Pacific Nuclear Test Area west of Hawaii, nuclear weapon manufacturing and quality assurance in Albuquerque, and inspection of nuclear and non-nuclear facilities throughout the country. He served with the 5th Air Force in Japan and later as a ranking Colonel, Officer in Charge of the Pacific Unified Command (TM)s alternate "command and control center" in Hawaii. In 1962, he was transferred and served as Deputy for Material for the 832 Air Division at Canon Air Force Base, Clovis, New Mexico. He retired from the USAF in 1964.

Did we go to the Moon? Colonel Dedrickson is a great example. Apollo 13 became known as the journey to the Moon that experienced technical difficulties, making it difficult and near impossible for the craft to return home.

According to Dedrickson: A spacecraft went to the rescue of Apollo 13, and they accompanied Apollo 13 on their voyage around the Moon back to Earth. And on two occasions they thought they might have to transfer the crew to their spacecraft, but they (the ET's) saw them safely back to Earth. His statements claimed extra-terrestrials would not allow the detonation of nuclear weapons on the Moon for our own scientific measurements. Former NASA Astronaut and Princeton physics professor, Dr Brian O'Leary (recruited by Carl Sagan to teach at Cornell University) had accused Sagan of being involved in covering up that information.

In mainstream disclosure this topic leaves no aspect of humanity untouched. If there is a secret space program, if governments have catalogued multiple species of beings, if there is new technology and new propulsion systems that "utilize the wheel work of nature," then how does one expect those who control the secrecy around this subject to simply disclose it? We should have had mass transparency from the very beginning, but this world of secrecy has developed so much that it's nearly impossible to get the entire truth out about multiple things within this subject. Technology, extra-terrestrial intelligence, and all of the questions you can think of have been the subject of inquiry for years, and we've been left completely in the dark. The largest benefit of disclosure could most possibly be the impact on human consciousness and awareness.

Adam's reading was interrupted by an excited murmur around the table. Outside they heard the thump of heavy footsteps. All eyes swivelled to the door expectantly. Imagination ran riot. Was a giant approaching? The door flung open to reveal Valdek, the one who had taken over at the last meeting. They had hoped it was a temporary arrangement. For once the grizzly old General was unsure of himself and slid down in his seat as low as he could. There was something really strange about this new arrival that disturbed him. Maybe he would not be noticed.

Adam stayed quiet. Valdek took his place and opened the folder before him. He looked contemptuously around the table and said, "This is a joke, I assume. Who put this together?"

An officer to his right put up his hand. "We have a special team collecting what information is getting to the public, through the internet, the media and elsewhere. We try to stop it of course."

Valdek grunted. "Not very successfully I see. Look at this." He thumbed the file and sorted to a page. Look at this, all of you."

Everyone there hastened to find the page he meant and read it.

Numerous claims have been made in recent years that support the result of one of the biggest security breaches in the history of the US military. According to reports, the US Navy and NASA have a fully operational Space Fleet. Interestingly, these 'accusations' are backed up by highly ranking individuals such as Senator Daniel K. Inouye who said: "There exists a ***shadowy government*** *with its own Air Force, its own Navy, its own fundraising mechanism, and the ability to pursue its own ideas of the national interest, free from all checks and balances, and free from the law itself."*

Valdek swore loudly. "This is like advertising our presence here. It cannot be allowed. Read on."

Top of Form
One of the best quotes regarding alien life and 'their' presence comes from Paul Hellyer, Former Canadian Defence Minister, and the man responsible for combining the Canadian Air Force, Army, and Navy into one united force, known as the Canadian Forces. Mr. Hellyer said: "Decades ago, visitors from other planets warned us about where we were headed and offered to help. But instead, we, or at least some of us, interpreted their visits as a threat and decided to shoot first and ask questions after... Trillions, and I mean thousands of billions of dollars have been spent on projects about which both the Congress and the Commander in Chief have been kept deliberately in the dark." But Hellyer isn't the only one who has ventured out to speak about alien life and the extra-terrestrial presence. In fact, numerous astronauts have done the same.

For a tense few moments there was absolute silence in the room. Suddenly a voice called out:

"Sir, if any of this is true then you are in trouble, aren't you, Sir?"

Valdek turned to face the speaker. "I am astonished at your ignorance and stupidity young man. You will be removed at once. Get him out of here."

Adam saw it was the red-haired young man from before. Once again, he wondered how he had ever been able to attend these meetings. It was a mystery to him. Where had he come from? He never ever saw him arrive. He was just inexplicably there and not one person queried his presence. The rest of the meeting was uneventful, and Adam had thankfully managed to keep a low profile.

***

Kate felt and looked extremely tired as a result of her energies being used to the full extent when she had deactivated the nuclear weapons. She kept dropping off to sleep even while eating. She noticed her father Jacob anxiously watching her. She knew of many others who worked with the spirit world who had overdone it and burnt themselves out. She realised her dad was worried that his daughter was going the same way. But after all, she reminded herself she did have that implant in her brain. That had to make a difference, didn't it?

Jacob put his hand on her shoulder. "Sweetheart I really think you need to have a rest from work. You will tire yourself out and then you will be no use to anybody. Why don't you take a little walk? It will do you good.

Kate shrugged her shoulders. "All right Dad. You are right, and a bit of fresh air is probably just what I need." It was early in the morning and the air was still fresh, waiting for the warmth of the sun. Kate pulled on a jacket and stepped out. She had earlier discovered a little stream that led to Senaka Creek, and she headed for that. She remembered that there was a wooden seat there where she could sit and could lose herself in her thoughts.

It was further along than she remembered and was glad to be able to rest there. The exercise and the rising sun had warmed her. She took her jacket off and leaned against the seat back. Soon she nodded off and slipped into dreamland, totally unaware that she was being watched. Due to the constant programming of her sessions into other worlds, without thinking and unconsciously she spoke her journey out loud to an invisible entity. The watcher edged closer, within earshot. This could turn out to be the proof he needed.

Kate's voice was soft and barely audible as she said, "What I am standing on is wet. It is similar to being in the flow of a stream, with smooth stones. The water is running, not still. Going down it is like stepping down an easy waterfall. Reminds me of the streams in Wales where the water tumbles over stones and ends up in a pool.

I am stepping down carefully. The water is quite warm and refreshing to my feet, which is lovely. There is nothing to hold onto. My legs are bare. I am not young in this as I can see by looking at my legs that I am not young. I go carefully, in case I fall. Each step takes me further into wherever I need to be in my subconscious. It is good.

I get to the bottom, and yes as I expected, there is a pool – not deep and the water is reasonably still. I am beginning to get a headache now. It is generally a sign of high connection for me. I try to loosen it off and yet stay connected. I keep going into higher vibrations. I follow the stream out of the pool. I feel a very strong connection. I don't know why I have to follow the stream in this way.

A voice tells me, "It is so you won't leave any traces behind, for where we are taking you we do not wish others to follow."

The stream twists and turns a little until I am told to step out onto the bank. I am in a very secret place. Nobody has been here from my world before. I am fully connected now. There are different kinds of beings from space here."

The watcher twitched with excitement, feeling frustrated that he could not see what Kate was seeing. He made sure his recording device was still working as he listened.

The voice said, "We work together. We do not work against each other, as you do on planet Earth. We work in harmony and for the betterment of all. If only humankind would follow our example, they would have an enlightened world instead of one where individuals are afraid to go out at night and walk the streets. How wonderful it would be if everybody could roam free with no fear, with no trepidation, but with the freedom of being anywhere they wish to be at any time and know that whoever they meet will be friendly towards them. Isn't that something to be sought?"

I certainly agree, but I don't see how telling me this can make the change.

"Hold in your mind this vision of people walking the streets freely, in happy communion with each other, even after dark, with no fear. See it in your mind." *(there followed a long stream of ET language*)."

The watcher almost fell over himself in excitement at the sounds that were coming out of the girl's mouth. He could hardly wait to get this back to Valdek and the team. He tried not to move for fear of waking her and bringing her out of trance. He was disappointed when though still in trance, she began to speak normally again.

"Why couldn't you give me this message at another time?"

"Your mind would not reach our communication unless you were in this relaxed subconscious state. This is why meditation is so important, to bring you to the levels we needed to communicate with you."

"I am not clear what you mean."

"We wish you to teach and stress to all, that meditation at a deep level is how everyone can find all the answers to their questions. Not only that, but they can discover what is really going on in their world. There would be no more secrets from them. They could manage their world, not the hidden Deep State. They just have to ask the questions of their subconscious to get the answers. It does not lie. It would mean the end of false information"

"I see. If you want answers you must ask the questions. You will not be told unless you ask."

"Exactly so. It is your job to pass this on, of course. Why else would you be here?"

The watcher could hardly contain himself. He got out his cameras. A photo of this was a must. The camera clicked. Immediately Kate jumped out of her trance. She knew she had been somewhere but could not remember where. Had she been dreaming? Gradually it all came back to her. She shook herself and stretched. It was time to go back to her father.

***

Silas called and called the number he had been given to reach Valdek. No matter how many times he tried to contact him he had no answer. Now he was worried. Had he been blocked, and what if Helga had badmouthed him? There was nothing she wouldn't do to get one over on him. Damn the woman, he said to himself, as he tried one more time to tell Valdek what he had. That would be a feather in his cap that Helga could not take off him.

Back in his apartment he sat on the bed, fuming inside. What could he do with the hot potato in his pocket? It had to go somewhere. He decided eventually to go to the only place he had an address for, building number seven, where the team of men surveyed the activities of people all over the world. They would know what to do, and most of all they would know how to contact Valdek. All previous addresses for meetings had been at hotels or rented places and so it was no use looking there.

An hour later he was in the dilapidated part of town, at door number seven. From appearances nobody outside would ever guess what went on beneath their feet. He keyed in the numbers needed on the pad and he was in. It unnerved him a bit when the door slammed shut behind him. He didn't remember it ever doing that before. Was that a draft of air he felt? Silas continued making his way very cautiously down the narrow stairs. A cockroach scurried out of his way across the boards. Treading along the uncarpeted passage he came to the door he had passed through on his earlier visit. His heart missed a beat when he saw it was already wide open, minus the press pad and eye scanner. He moved warily into the room. All the desks, monitors, screens on walls were all gone. Investigating further, he found the same thing in all rooms along the corridor. Everything that had ever been there was gone, cleared out. His heart pumped so hard he had to lean against a wall for support. He wondered if he going to have a heart attack.

He took several minutes trying to control his trembling legs before he found that he could stand without the support of the wall. What did this all mean? Why hadn't anyone warned him? Feeling sick and shaky he stumbled out of the building into the deserted street. What to do now? He had no idea. Against his will and better judgement he knew he needed to get in touch with Helga to see if she had been notified, or if it was only himself that had been kept out of the loop.

CHAPTER ELEVEN

FUTURE WORLD

The way forward. Look for the way forward. If you are looking you will see it. It is evident and not at all hidden. Seek out the Wisdoms of the Ages which lie within you. If you look far enough, you will also see a long way into the future time. All is the same, no past, no present and no future separation. It is all together in you.

Erasmus

Kate again took advantage of Adam's absence to have a deep meditation by herself. She had almost forgotten to engage in this way since her journeys nowadays were monitored and watched over by her friends. It wasn't that she minded so much, but it was nice to have more privacy from time to time.

As always, she talked through it and recorded on a device so that she didn't need to try to remember afterwards – it was all there.

"I am walking on sharp jagged rock, like flints stood up on end. There are places where I can put my feet, but it is not easy to walk through. I don't know what this is telling me, but I'm not going down steps as I usually do and am on the flat. I keep going forward, what else can I do? I see a blue haze in the distance. There is a strange blueness in the sky, not a natural one but one that is reflected from something. I move towards the haze to see what it is. It is a really peculiar blue, an unnatural blue, an electric blue. I am winding my way forward very carefully, but I am not alone now.

There are other things here, moving and living in these sharp up-ended rocks. Little creatures, perhaps lizards. I don't know. Oh, they are not lizards, they look humanoid. Interesting because they look like little Greys and yet I know they are not Greys, but little people. They live quite naturally in these rocks. It is easy for them because they are small. They move along with me, as if to see where I will go and to keep me company as I go.

I don't know where this is taking me. I get nearer to where the blue light is coming from, I have to use my Earth words. It is coming from a big city and the blue is the lighting of that city. Normally we on Earth would have white light colour, but this is blue. This is a different city to what we are used to. It is something that is coming to our time. Or rather we are coming to its time. The area is busy. As I get closer into the city itself, I see streets are such as we normally have and not so different, and vehicles that I haven't seen before, but everything seems to be powered with a blue light. This is not a natural light. I suppose you could say it is like electricity but comes with a blue rather than a white light.

"Why is this?" I ask.

I get a response. "This is the means by which your world will be fuelled, be energised. We receive energy by means of this light. It is simply a different mechanism to one you have been used to. It is perfectly adequate. The blue does have an effect on the mood of the people. They will be different. They will be adjusted and accustomed to this. So because of that it is not harmful to them. This is for the future, not for your current days. If we were to introduce this means of power now the human body would not have time to adjust to it. It will be introduced gradually over the coming years. You may sense or see a change in the colour of your light supply, or light that comes from any energy source that is being used. Experiments are already underway for use of this alternative to what you currently use."

"Wow! Is this going to be harmful?"

"No, simply an adjustment that has been used on other worlds."

"I keep getting words I can't understand here. How does this relate to our situation currently with all the wars?"

"Sooner rather than later many will come to realise that fighting each other is not the answer and that bonding together will be your salvation."

"I like that."

"You will be fewer in numbers however. That in itself is a salvation. The time we have shown you is drawing near for the world now. The time is drawing near and is close enough for your scientists to see it coming. It is no longer way ahead in the far future. There will be signs. Some of you may call them portents or even omens. The signs will be unmistakeable and will be seen throughout the world by all, not just those who focus on these things. We will make our presence felt; comfortably it is to be hoped. Diehards will resist acknowledging what they see. There will be what you call cognitivc dissonance when many more events surface. It is important to recognise this since not everybody will be of the same mind and you may wonder at this."

"Thank you." It ended abruptly just as if the line had been cut.

Kate had much to think about and share.

***

Kate felt she was on a roll. Why was she getting so much information, and without asking for it? It was as if they wanted to give as much as possible while they had a chance. Why the rush? Was it because of the wedding, or something else more sinister? Who was giving her all this stuff and what was she to do with it? She needed to ask her father. Maybe he would know, especially as he was awakening very fast now, much more than before. She wondered if Master M had a programme or a time limit. Was it to do with the advancement of the Human Race as indicated by The Golden One at the last Galactic meeting?

Before she had a chance to ask she found herself in another experience, again recorded.

"I go down very steep stairs, and I feel as if I'm going down into a basement. It is very dark. I can't really see. I come to a trap door taking me even further down. These are steps rather than stairs. I don't know what to call them. They are more solid. I still can't see what's at the bottom. I must go down, to follow what they've given me. I can hear light music as if in a distance, so I can just catch the sound of it. I walk towards the sound. The walls are closed in and I can touch both sides to feel what they are made of. They are of mud. At the bottom there is a very narrow, long and twisted path. I still can't see where I am going, just the bit I am walking on. I have a blocked area in front of me, a wall of some kind. There must be a way forward or I would not have been brought here. I push on the wall and it swings on a pivot. I walk through to the other side and it swings shut behind me. There's more light now and I can see at last. I sense this place is inhabited, that something lives here. The air is sweet, comfortable, warm and feels cosy, homely. I could be comfortable here. There's nobody around yet, but someone must come surely. Then two little dogs come running up to me. There has to be someone here. Who looks after them?

A man arrives. His clothes are not manufactured, they are stitched together. Natural material. He puts his hand out for me to shake. There is a nice feeling to his hand.

He says in a soft quiet voice, as if he was expecting me. "You have come in by the back door, by the back entrance that nobody knows about. Now you will come with me to the regular living quarters for we cannot take you to the main entrance. The legitimate entrance is monitored and patrolled. You have managed to get in by the back door. Well done."

I go along with him. He is not tall. I trot alongside him for he has long strides and is faster than me. We go past several doors; it is too much to call them offices, but I can see they are for official use and are also storerooms. We have not yet come to the living quarters. The stores are of this and that, all crated. I cannot see what is inside but there are labels attached to the crates. I rush to catch up with him. He stops every so often and waits for me to get my breath. He is going so fast.

The air is still nice and sweet. We come to doors which are operated by locks, not those with a key but keypad locks where you have to key in a number. The door opens. As we step through it closes silently behind. I notice a few other ordinary looking people around. There are some stairs, some going down, some going up, to what I feel are departments. We come to what I call a pretty door, done up to make it look sweet. We go in and there are groups of children learning, reading, studying, painting. They have activities that will keep them occupied while being monitored by adults, both male and female. They look human, but very pale, which may be because there is no natural sunlight.

He takes me to an office with a desk and chairs. How they got the chairs down here I don't know.

He picks up my thought. "It is not important for you to know. There is a lot you have not seen yet, but what we have shown you so far you can report on. Put it down for the records. You *must* put it down for the record, for if for any reason this place ceases to exist you will have a record of it to take to the surface. Our existence here is not guaranteed. We will hold on to this lifestyle for as long as we can, but continuation of it is not guaranteed. We do not know what will happen in the future, so you must make a record of this to keep safe on the surface."

I thank him as I come back. I wake up in my bed. It seems apparent they are expecting something to happen and in telling me this it will not be unknown or forgotten. I wonder about our future together as a species of humanity.

While Kate pondered on the experience and message given, she heard clearly in her head.

Reflect on the humble beginnings of so many, of past great men and women on your planet who have changed the destinies of us all.

She wondered who in the future this might be. Perhaps one of those children studying underground, being looked after for later times.

***

Kate was very disturbed because she felt there was no time left to pass on the information. Things seemed to be speeding up, was the end coming after all? And what was it that she had not seen yet? How much more could she take?

Adam arrived home some hours later and could tell straight away that Kate was troubled.

"Darling, what's with that long face? Are you getting fed up with waiting for the wedding? It won't be long, I promise."

"It's not that Adam. Every time I sit down and relax I drift off to sleep and I am taken into a deep state and given more information. I don't know what to do with it all. Listen, it is even recorded for me. I feel I am taken away somewhere unknown."

Adam frowned. He was puzzled as this wasn't like Kate at all. He needed time to think. "Let's all have a meal first then you can share it with both your father and I. Between us we can come up with answers I am sure.

An hour later seated in the garden they all listened to the recordings which were amazingly clear.

"Well what do you think?" Kate asked. "I don't know if I can go on much longer. It has all become too much and it doesn't matter anymore who my grandfather is. What if I stopped now, right now? The world would still continue, people in the streets would carry on with their personal situations, no matter what that might mean. I too am entitled to a private life, aren't I? Well, aren't I?"

Jacob looked at her appalled. "Darling girl. You can't stop now. What about Adam, what about the wonderful time travelling team Jamère and Sechem? They all expect you to follow through."

Kate pulled on her father's hand. "Dad, you are coming on so fast now. Perhaps you can take my place."

"Never, ever. Don't even think about it."

She wiped her tears. Her father was right. It was no good thinking anymore. If the balance didn't swing in favour of being a more loving human on Earth, the end was near anyway. Earth as she knew it would be gone for ever and creatures like Gork and Valdek would rule.

***

Kate was not going to be allowed to stop, however much she wanted to. That same night they took her again. Who were *they?* That question would not be answered until much later.

She felt she was between two worlds as she dropped off to sleep. Just before oblivion she heard the distinctive click of the digital recorder. She was off again into another world.

"I am on a zig zag path. There are a lot of meanings to that. Each turn gives a different viewpoint. A zigzag path takes longer but reaches higher. Oh yes!

Before me I see a five-bar gate, easily opened, but I must remember to close it behind me. I come to a flat grassy plain which seems to go on for ever. "What is this telling me?"

At the side is a path and along it comes a little old man. I assume old because he is bent over and holding on to a stick. He has been around for a very long time. He comes up to me and takes my hand.

"Where do you want to go, girl?"

"I want to go somewhere that has some meaning, that gives me some information."

"Well you'd best come with me then."

So I follow him. He is not very big. His age has made him small, but he is all there in his head. He leads me along a path, a country, farmyard type path. He knows where he is going, but I don't. We come to a barn. People are in there sitting around a table, talking. There is a mixture of male and female.

"We are making plans for the harvest."

"Oh, where do I come into this? Why am I here?"

"We are harvesting what you have been sowing. We are harvesting what you have been growing. The time is coming near when we will gather all the bits you have given us. We will put it to good use."

"I am not very clear on this?"

"Everything you've learnt, everything you have helped others to understand and learn have all been seeds and will become meaningful when we harvest. For we gather in what has been learnt and store it for future generations. What you have been sowing will be there for the future when there is a need. There will be necessity then for this information in the words you have put out and in the changes you have made. When there is a need, they will be there in the storehouse that we are preparing. We will look after it. We will make sure it doesn't go to rot and doesn't lie forgotten anywhere. The harvest will be good. Believe it, don't doubt. That is all you have to do right now. Believe in yourself and what you are doing."

Kate slept on.

***

In Dorset it was getting dark, but the birds were still singing, making their last calls before settling down for the night. A blackbird's song echoed through the trees. An owl hooted in the gathering dusk. Poppy pulled off her boots and put them aside after walking the dogs.

"Settle down boys. That is your lot for the day."

They looked at her with soulful eyes and knew she meant it. Poppy sighed a heavy sigh. There was not much doing in her part of the woods in Dorset. It wasn't that she looked for excitement, but she so very much missed her friend Kate since she left and tied up with Adam. Would she ever see her again?

It had certainly been exciting when the men in dark suits had visited her after Kate had disappeared so suddenly. But she wasn't able to tell them where Kate was because she didn't know. The last thing that happened that shook her view of reality was when Kate and Jacob simply vanished from her home. One minute they were there and the next they vanished. How did they do that? How could she explain that to her own mind?

Poppy opened her computer, as she did every evening before she cooked her meal. Maybe, just maybe she would get an email or message from her friend explaining things. The screen came alive. There in bold lettering was the message she had hoped and longed for. Her heart jumped in delight. Perhaps Kate was right when she said, 'put your thoughts on what you want, and it will manifest'.

Hello dear friend. I have missed you so much. Adam and I are to marry, and we want you to come over for the wedding. Will you? It will be in Washington DC. Date to be arranged. Get yourself a passport. Tickets for flights will be arranged and sent to you and we will meet you at the airport. More later.

Oh, and by the way, Francine is also invited. Sorry about that. If we can we'll put you on different flights. Must keep this short M.I.B. you know – ha ha. Much love Kate. XXX

Poppy didn't know when she had felt so happy. She was going to see her friend again. Then she started to worry. Who would look after the dogs while she was away? How did one go about getting a passport? She would need a photo, wouldn't she? Oh, and she absolutely had to get a new outfit. So much to arrange. Questions buzzed around and around in her head until at last she fell asleep.

CHAPTER TWELVE

REMOTE VIEWING

The best way to predict the future is to create it.
Abraham Lincoln

Once more Kate played the recording of the last journey, what she now called 'the unknown'. As Jacob and Adam sat listening they heard a scrabbling sound coming from the window. She stopped the tape as her father went to investigate.

Jacob soon returned, laughing like crazy. "It's those two devils Sechem and Jamère up to their tricks."

"For heaven's sake tell them to come in and stop messing about," Adam said. "What do they want this time?"

At once both Time Travellers appeared in the room. "We were just practising," Sechem said. "We must not get rusty."

Into Kate's head came the image of The Tin Man in the film 'Wizard of Oz'. She laughed. These two were certainly not rusty tin men.

"I have a question to ask Kate," said Jamère as he perched himself on the arm of the settee. "Kate, you did do a remote viewing course, didn't you?"

"Well yes, but it was quite some time ago now, way back in Dorset. Why do you ask?" Kate was suspicious. He never asked anything without a reason. What was coming next? "Why bring this up now with so much else going on? And we still haven't sorted out arrangements for our wedding."

Sechem's whole demeaner took on an air of excitement. Kate recognised that cheeky look. What was he planning now? Sechem grinned, grabbed Jamère and together they did a little dance around the room.

"Oh, we have plenty of time for that. Official papers and red tape, they all have to go through a lengthy process, don't they? What we want you to do can be done in an afternoon."

"No more, please." Kate began to cry. "Enough is enough."

Adam lifted her chin with his hand. "Darling how can you doubt what you can do after listening to that last recording? Everything you have done so far is invaluable and will be so for a long time. This is only one afternoon."

She looked at him, loving him so much. "Are you in on this Adam? What is it they want me to do? What if I fail?" she frowned.

"Hold on, hold on. All these questions. Please relax darling. It is just a little job. It won't take long."

Kate sighed she knew from experience how something innocuous could turn into something big. What is it you want me to do?" she repeated.

Adam waved to Sechem to keep quiet and stay still for once. "Stop jigging around. You are making me feel giddy." Sechem pulled a face but the gleam in his eye was still clear to Kate.

Adam turned her to face him. "Darling there is an important meeting to be held at Dulce military base in New Mexico tomorrow afternoon and we want you to be there."

Jacob grabbed Adam by the arm. "You can't send her there. She mustn't get involved with that awful place. I have researched what has gone on there in the past. It is not safe for her." His grip tightened on Adam's arm. "This is what I found out about the place. I don't know if any of it is true, but it sounds convincing enough for anyone to need to stay clear."

Adam released his arm, from Jacob's tight grasp. "I've heard it all too, but she will be safe."

Jacob would not be put off. “Listen, this is what I read Adam - On the surface, Dulce is just a small southwestern town, but according to rumours, it’s just a cap on a large underground facility which is home to unimaginable experiments and technologies. There is a whole world underneath Dulce — a secret, high-tech one filled with aliens.

“According to some, the Dulce subterranean base is at least a seven-story compound beneath Dulce, that houses human-animal hybrids, human-alien hybrids, and extremely advanced technologies. Philip Schneider, a former explosive engineer employed by the U.S. government, said that Dulce was a site of a brutal human-alien war. Schneider, who had high-level security clearance, claimed that he helped construct a “secret underground base” in Dulce in 1979. He said he witnessed a battle with subterranean aliens that left 60 humans dead. The alien war wages even now. Phil Schneider said he was working as an explosive’s expert, helping build secret underground bases for the U.S. government in Dulce, N.M., in 1979. Schneider was suspicious about the underground base he was helping to build when he saw so many Special Forces Green Berets around camp.

“In 1995, he told of his encounter with alien beings living underground. Schneider said he was one of three survivors in a battle with aliens in August 1979 and that he was the only person with a high-level security clearance speaking out in such detail about the government’s knowledge of alien beings. He explained that when the work team drilled four large holes, the standard way to start construction, what emerged from the holes was not at all part of standard procedure. Black sooty air came up when we drilled holes there.”

Kate gasped, horrified. “That sounds like the Black Goo the giant told me about. I don’t want to go anywhere near that.”

"Just listen," Jacob said. "Schneider said this in a lecture at the 1995 Preparedness Expo. Furthermore when he went underground to make an assessment, he found himself just feet away from a "big Grey"—a 7-foot-tall alien. The stench was worse than the worst garbage. The entity was absolutely horrible, he said. Schneider told how he fumbled for a pistol and killed two of the beings, but not before one of them emitted a strange and harmful energy.

"He showed the audience his hand. The beam had burned off some of the fingers on his left hand and hit his chest. It had also burned his shoes off and even burned his toenails off. A Green Beret saved Schneider's life and lost his own in the process. He got Schneider into a lift and pushed the button to raise him above ground to safety.

"More than 60 people lost their lives that day, said Schneider. The other two survivors are living in nursing homes in Canada, protected by the Canadian government, and no American citizen is allowed access to them. Schneider said this is because they were scared of being kidnapped. There's a war under there and it's been going on ever since," he said. He spoke of 1,477 underground bases around the world, 129 of which were located in the United States. Each cost $17 billion or more. He said the Black Budget, hidden from other U.S. government agencies and from the public, garners 25 percent of the gross national product. Military forces from multiple countries have been engaged in such warfare with aliens, he said

"Preceding his death in 1997 Schneider claimed multiple attempts were made on his life after he began revealing what he knew. His death by suicide has been viewed with suspicion by his supporters."

"Is that enough to convince you Adam? It should be."

"Jacob, calm down. I am not sending Kate there in person. I wouldn't be so foolish. She is going to a meeting on the surface, not underground."

Kate had been listening with growing dismay. It was her turn to have a say.

"Are you mad? Why would I, a nobody be invited anyway? It doesn't make sense."

Both Sechem and Jamère laughed like crazy. "A *no-body*, that's a good one."

"Oh, for heaven's sake, get to the point." Kate was infuriated.

They collapsed, laughing harder than ever. "*for heaven's sake.* Oh my stars!"

Kate had had enough. "I'm leaving, since you'll never get around to telling me what this is all about."

"Alright my darling. What we want you to do is just to remote view that meeting and report back. Not go there physically."

"Surely Sechem can do that?" Kate was puzzled. "It seems he can go anywhere."

Sechem pulled a long face. "No, dear friend. This work has to be done by a citizen of Earth as we have repeatedly told you. The report has to be passed on, by you through Adam. Will you do it?"

"You know I can't say no if it is so important."

Adam said, "Oh, I know it is important and very hush hush since I am not invited. It is way above my level of need to know." However, an anxious look came over his face.

Kate gave a huge sigh. "Alright. I'll do it."

They settled Kate into a comfortable chair and allowed her time to go into herself.

"Will it work?" Jacob asked. "She hasn't done this for a very long time."

"This time she has a target, whereas her other journeys have been random to some extent. Have faith Jacob." Sechem said. "As before she will report as she goes. If she doesn't she will have forgotten everything after she returns."

They settled down to wait. After a short while, before their eyes Kate began to lose form, something her father could never get used to, even though he knew the procedure of changing dimensions.

After a few moments Kate began her report on the meeting. "I'm in a room, it is very plush with deep, soft green leather office chairs. Glasses and water are set out on a highly polished table. There are – let me count – there are twelve men here. They have an air about them of confident authority and appear to be in accord with each other. There can't be any psychics here or they would see me. That is a relief.

"Oh, now this *is* a surprise. I discover that my energy has entered the physical form of a tea trolley. I didn't tell it to do that, it just did." Kate let out a nervous laugh. "I've never been a tea trolley before. I wonder if other spirit forms can do that."

"Keep your mind on your job," reminded Sechem.

"Hey, my goodness, just listen to what they are saying," Kate cried. "The subject is de-population. I repeat, listen to this.

"You know we can't hear them. You will have to tell us what they are saying," Sechem said.

"Oh yes, I forgot. A white-haired Saville Row suited man of later years leans forward in his chair and is making a statement. He has a gold earring in one ear and a gold ring on his left hand. What thick sausage fingers he has too. But he is strong, very strong and I wouldn't mess with him for a moment. I am glad he can't see me, but he is looking in an odd manner towards the tea trolley. Oh my goodness, I feel very peculiar as his energy reaches me. I remember the saying, *energy flows where attention goes.* Listen, they are speaking again.

"*The plan will work very well. A virus is the quickest and most financially viable method. It can spread globally, and so fast with all the constant air travel. This is quicker than war, and no blame will be placed on any one country. A perfect solution for reducing numbers.*

"A swarthy skinned man with wonderful teeth speaks next. *I agree. It will affect babies and children most. An ideal solution.*

"A red-cheeked portly man, clearly from the affluent western world is speaking now.

"I suggest it be introduced into countries that are already highly overpopulated and where childbearing is a must in their culture. A lot of those countries have aid programmes with aid workers. Those same aid workers will be the ones to spread the virus. Yes, it's a good plan."

One by one those around the table are making agreeable noises except for two men. A grey-haired man who appears to be in his mid-fifties hesitates and seems afraid to speak out. He coughs loudly, out of nerves I feel.

"Have any of you considered that your own families could be affected by this virus once it got hold? Furthermore, if you yourselves became ill for any reason, the very medics you rely on might also be affected and therefore not available to you. If only out of self-interest, we should consider that."

A tailor suited, dark-haired man said, "Excuse me. That is already covered. I heard that if there is a danger of this kind, or any real danger to us, many would take personal doctors or nurses with them on their flights, to treat them and their families in the event that they became infected. The wealthy would also be besieging doctors in private clinics in Harley Street, London, and across the world. If rich enough they would use private jets to set off for holiday homes or specially prepared disaster bunkers in countries that would appear to avoid the worst of any virus outbreak."

Silence follows for a full five long minutes.

"Sechem, it seems they are really taking in that possibility."

The younger of the two men is getting to his feet and says. "I vote we hold off for a while until we get a higher authority agreement. All in favour?"

The Saville Row suited man is still staring hard at the trolley. I feel most uncomfortable and unsafe. He is getting up from the table and walking towards it. If he gets too close, he will enter my energy field. I am scared now. Sechem, I can't hold this any longer. I have to leave."

Slowly, very slowly Kate resumed her form in the chair. The four men were silent as they took in the implications of what they had heard. It was unthinkable that any force on Earth would do such a thing as releasing a virus so devastating. Had they thought about the suffering that would bring? This could be worse than the Great Plague.

CHAPTER THIRTEEN

THE WEDDING

Sit still and wait and great things will happen. This is the equivalent of a drum roll for you all. There is never a drum roll for undesirable events but always for a great moment, an exciting moment. Wait with bated breath and joy in your heart. This event will change your life, all life forever.

Kate stirred at first light. Something had woken her. Then she heard it, the loud call of an owl. There must be many owls in this area of Bethesda she reflected. As much as she tried, she couldn't get back to sleep. She hoped that Sechem and Jamère would not call on her for any more tasks before the wedding. The ceremony was to be a small affair with her father Jacob, her surrogate mother Francine, The General and of course her dearest friend, Poppy. She could hardly contain herself at the thought of seeing her again. It was such a long time since she first saw Adam at a lecture in Dorset and when she fell in love straight away.

Everything had fallen into place and her world had never been the same since. The official papers had been cleared and Adam had sent off the plane tickets to arrive in plenty of time. Poppy would be with her very soon. She wished with all her heart that Poppy could see Sechem, Jamère and Master M as she did. Her invisible friends were certain to be attending and all should go smoothly. What could go wrong?

***

Excitement filled the air in Poppy's house too. It crackled with electricity as Poppy made arrangements for her cherished dogs to have a trusted friend live in and look after them while she was away. She would only be gone for one week after all. *You'll be alright*, she told them daily as she looked at their anxious faces. They sensed that something was going on, and it wasn't anything they wanted. They watched their beloved mistress as she tried on several outfits, none of which they had seen her wear before. Boris, the large wolfhound, never left her side and whined pitifully. Poppy absentmindedly patted him as she pored over the flight tickets and contact details. She wanted to be sure that all was in order and that nothing could go wrong.

The day came at last. She kissed each dog in turn and got into the waiting taxi. Although it wasn't ideal, she had arranged to meet Francine at Heathrow. They were after all to travel on the same plane. It was the best Adam could do in the time. Poppy had never flown before, and Francine, as a well-travelled lady, could show her the ropes. They both had to get along for Kate's sake.

Poppy eyed Francine up and down as they met and felt inadequate for a moment. I'm as good as she is, she told herself. Clothes do not make the woman. They boarded the plane together in silence.

***

Kate could hardly keep still, hopping from one foot to the other as she watched the passengers coming out of the exit into the arrival's hall, pushing their trolleys before them. Then she saw them. Dignified, elegant Francine came first, looking like a celebrity. Then shorter, plump, darling Poppy followed on behind, puffing slightly. Kate's face lit up as she rushed to greet them. She threw her arms around her friend, before giving a peck on the cheek to her mother.

"I have a car waiting," she told them. "We'll be home soon." Threading their way through the traffic, they were soon at Adam's house.

"Very nice indeed," sniffed Francine. "You have had done well after all, daughter.

Kate could see how her mother was thinking and hoped she was wrong. She sensed she would love to come and live here too since her current husband was boring and past his best. As Kate picked up her mother's thoughts she said, "Don't even think about it mother."

Francine gasped. "I never said anything, Kate."

Poppy was equally impressed with the surroundings. "I'm so happy for you Kate. I really am, even though you are so far away from me."

"You can come and visit me whenever you want," said Kate giving her a warm hug.

They soon settled into their rooms, and that evening when Adam came home they sat outside drinking comfortably together in the warm evening air, going over the arrangements for the following days.

"What's that noise?" Francine looked around, startled.

"It's only an owl," said Kate and Poppy together. "it seems there are a lot round here."

"There is a saying among the indigenous people that when an owl calls your name it means a death," said Adam.

Francine snorted. "I don't hear a name," she said. "Superstition, that's what it is."

Nobody bothered to follow with a comment. It wasn't worth the effort. Even so a chill passed through Kate.

***

The wedding day drew near. It was to be a small private ceremony, held at the old General's insistence in the extensive grounds of his house in the McClean district, home to many diplomats, businesspeople, members of Congress, and high-ranking government officials, partially due to its proximity to Washington, D.C. and the Central Intelligence Agency. The district of McLean is often distinguished by its luxury homes and is said to be the third wealthiest district in the United States.

"Why does it have to be there?" Kate asked. "Are you so afraid of him that you have to obey, even if you prefer it to be at your home?"

Adam busied himself with some papers before replying. Kate knew it was a delaying tactic she had seen him use before while he thought of an appropriate answer.

"Darling, we wouldn't be getting married if the old man hadn't got all the obligatory documents that were indispensable, passed through and stamped. He has the clout and contacts that we needed. Apart from that sweetheart, aren't you forgetting the reason I am here on this Earth as Colonel Adam Fenshawe? Now as a human Trojan Horse I may be able to stop some of the disastrous actions of the Shadow Government. Staying in the General's good books is vital. As I said, he may be old, but he has influence. We will be safe under his umbrella."

Kate listened to his logic and couldn't help but agree. She sighed as she stood by him at his desk. She hugged him and kissed the top of his head.

"Darling, you do know that his property is almost on top of the headquarters of the C.I.A.? That is a bit too close for comfort in my mind. His power doesn't stretch that far."

Adam frowned and bit his lip. It would all go well. He knew it would.

***

The day arrived. It was a beautiful day with a clear blue sky. Kate stretched her arms and breathed deeply. She could hear her father snoring in the room across the landing. At least Poppy and Francine were too far away to be disturbed by him. It was going to be a good day, she felt it in her bones. It was still early but the birds were up singing their hearts out. She headed for the kitchen smiling happily.

"Oh, I see you are enjoying life." It was Sechem leaning against the wall. "Come out Jamère, she won't bite." A flash of blue erupted from a cupboard and Jamère emerged with a huge grin on his face.

Kate laughed with them. It was so good to see them arrive. She wasn't sure they would be able to come since they usually only arrived when there was work for her to do.

"Now you are sure nobody will see you, aren't you?" she asked.

"Unless you have invited a bunch of psychics, nobody will see us." Sechem said.

"Well, my Dad will since he is advancing rapidly with his abilities and he wasn't bad before. Jamère, don't play any of your mad tricks, will you? Promise me."

"How about some fireworks?" he asked.

Kate wagged her finger at him and laughed. "Go now and let me get ready."

Everybody was busy with the preparations. There was a moment early in the afternoon just before the ceremony when Adam looked into the trees surrounding the property and saw something that made him stop short in surprise. It couldn't be, could it? Almost obscured by the branches was the red-haired young man who caused disruption at the secret meetings. He appeared to be hiding, but why or how was he there? Adam strode towards the trees to ask but as he did so the young man ran off. Adam shrugged his shoulders and did not pursue. He had other things to focus on.

The wedding went without a hitch. The old General did them proud and Adam soon realised that the old trouper was treating him as the son he had lost and was to be trusted. It humbled and pleased Adam.

After the ceremony he frowned as he watched Francine making up to the old man. Who knew what was in her head? He could only guess. The fact that the General was so much older than her would not stop her, and as a wealthy widower he was a catch. Would she ever stop interfering? He doubted it, and he knew the General would be flattered by the attention she was giving him. There is no fool like an old fool, as the saying goes.

Jacob was also watching Francine and sensed her intentions. The poor old guy, medals or not had no chance against her advances. He decided to let it go. What will be will be, and they were both old enough to decide for themselves.

Adam watched the various expressions on Jacob's face. He saw there such a mixture of joy and pride, but also anxiety. They were fleeting insights into what might be going on in his head. He had been thrown into an unfamiliar world with very little say in his future. Adam loved his father in law and vowed to make sure he was happy. In the meantime there was still so much to organise for Poppy's stay. They had agreed together that the honeymoon would be postponed until Poppy and Francine returned to England.

***

Newly married Kate sat reading the morning papers and looked up as Poppy came in wearing jeans and T shirt.

"Poppy what would you like to do today? We must make your few days here memorable," Kate said as she folded the paper.

"You should be on your honeymoon," Poppy said.

"That will come later. I want to make the most of you while you are here." Kate smiled at her friend. It was so good to have her close at this most important stage in her life. Next moment Francine walked in, unsteady on her feet and looking a little worse for wear.

Kate hid an amused smile. "Good night?" she asked her mother. All she got in response was a grunt. Her mother was never a morning person.

Kate attempted to brighten her mood up a little. "Adam has to go into town today. How about we three go shopping? It will be fun, and you can get clothes you can't buy in England."

Francine grimaced. "A bit later, tomorrow perhaps. I am having coffee with the General and he is picking me up."

"Just you and I then Poppy. OK, we'll use my car, but Adam said we can use Joe, his driver. I don't want to drive myself until I get used to DC traffic."

***

Poppy enjoyed the comfort of the Buick as she sat alongside Kate. This was so different to the 4 x 4's she used in Dorset to drive around the country and get all her dogs on board. This was luxury and there was no need to worry about getting dirt on her clothes. She gave a contented sigh as she leaned back against the softness of the seat.

Kate gave her a hug. "We'll go to the Westfield Montgomery Mall, but first I need to pick up some dry cleaning. Joe can take you to the Mall and I'll meet you outside Macy's at 10.00 am. Is that alright with you, Poppy? I'll take a cab there.

"Poppy smiled. "Joe will look after me I'm sure, Kate."

Joe pulled up and she watched Kate quickly hop out of the car and disappear into the crowd.

"Onwards, Joe," she laughed. This was fun.

They joined the freeway, keeping to the set speed. Poppy noted how everybody seemed to know where they were going.

"I'm glad I am not driving," she told Joe. "I'd be lost immediately."

"Yes, Ma-am," he said. It is best to know the area. We'll be leaving the freeway soon."

Neither of them saw the black car coming until the last moment. There was an almighty crunching, grinding noise and their car flipped over and over. It came to rest on its side. No sound came from within.

***

Kate waited and waited at the Mall at the agreed meeting place. It was past 10.00 am, the agreed meeting time. Where was Poppy? Surely she couldn't be lost. After all she had Joe to make sure she was in the right place. She phoned his mobile. No answer. It was then she saw it. The view on the TV in the shop window was crystal clear. There it was, number plate of a car on its side in full view. It was her car. Her heart plummeted with shock. She stood motionless for what seemed to be an eternity. Shaking with dread she called a cab. She had to get to Adam and hoped he might be home by now.

Adam at that moment was standing stock still in front of the TV. Starkly clear on the screen was Kate's car, badly damaged. He froze. The newsreader was saying,

"There were no survivors."

This couldn't be true. Joe was an excellent driver, one of the best. This had to be a mistake.

He called out to Jacob. "Come here, now. Tell me that Kate and Poppy changed their minds and didn't go shopping." His hands couldn't stop shaking. What should he do? Phone the police?

Jacob came into the room, tears streaming down his cheeks. “The Owl called her name,” he said. He sat down heavily and buried his heads in his hands.

“Jacob, Jacob, Pull yourself together. Tell me they are alright. It can’t be true. They walked away from this, didn’t they?”

Jacob looked up, his eyes red. “The Owl called her name,” he repeated. “Whatever will I do now?”

They heard the cab pull up and both tensed as they heard the door opening. In walked Kate, still shaking like a leaf about to fall from the tree. She fell into Adam’s arms.

“Tell me it isn’t true,” she said, her voice caught in a sob. “Tell me it isn’t Poppy in that crash. What about Joe? Have you heard anything from him?”

“Thank goodness you are alright.” Adam wrapped his arms around her. Tears ran down his face. He could have lost her.

Jacob sat motionless muttering to himself. “The Owl called her name. What will happen now Adam? Oh, Poppy.”

Kate, you had better give him a whisky while I find out about Poppy and Joe.” Adam excused himself and went to make the calls from another room. In his heart he sensed that this was no accident and that Kate was the intended victim. It was her car and she could have been driving. Where were Sechem and Jamère?

***

Adam waited anxiously for the return to his calls. Even so he still jumped when the phone rang.

It was a voice he had heard before, but not one he was expecting. “Sir, are you alone?”

Adam recognised the voice of the red-haired youth who had caused disruption at the meetings, and strangest of all, who had hidden behind the trees at the wedding. How on earth did he get this phone number and why was he calling him at this critical time?

"Sir, are you alone?" he repeated. There was an urgent tone to his voice.

"Your wife is in danger. After your next phone calls meet me outside three houses down and I will explain." The phone went dead. Adam shook his head. Did that really happen? Then the phone rang again, it was the police. Adam listened to their news and returned to the other room and told them to wait as he had urgent business to attend to. He quickly left the house.

It had grown dark by this time as he walked the few houses, looking right and left as he went. Suddenly a hand grabbed his arm and pulled him aside into the bushes.

"Be quiet," he was commanded. "You know me?" Adam nodded.

"I am not what you think I am, the red-haired idiot." Adam nodded again.

"So, who and what are you?"

"I come and go as I please, from one dimension to another. You understand me? I am not as you are, fully in the flesh, but I can move between." He looked very hard at Adam. "***Do*** you understand what I am saying?"

Adam swallowed hard. "Yes," he croaked. "You are a Time Traveller?"

The young man smiled. "Got it in one. Now your young lady must be monitored, kept safe. There are forces who are out to get her. She *must* not die. Got it?"

Adam tried to get a hold on the young man to ask more, but he was not there anymore. He was gone. Adam walked slowly back to his house.

***

In a dark street a little distance from US naval academy in Annapolis, Maryland, and north of the Medical Centre, there was a quiet celebration. In spite of the surveillance team's hurried evacuation from number 7, the new building suited them perfectly, even better than before. The team's operator picked up the phone. Valdek had to be told.

"Mission accomplished, sir. We tracked her car as she left Bethesda with her friend. It was all too easy since we had placed our remote tracker on the vehicle. It made one brief stop, and then our man did the work." He paused while he listened.

"No sir, there were no survivors." The operator heard a low grunt of pleasure.

"It took you long enough. Why didn't you get the man too? You should not have allowed them to get married." The phone slammed down.

There was no satisfying Valdek the operator decided. A least Helga and Silas would be pleased and get off his back. It was then with a shock that he realised he hadn't told those bothersome two of the relocation to the new premises. Oops! He picked up the phone again. Some excuse would be needed.

***

Two hours later, Valdek stormed around a darkened room in a hotel off Capitol Hill, knocking over chairs as he rampaged. A small team of men cowered by the door and kept their eyes lowered. They tried hard not to make eye contact in case this would invite more of the creature's wrath.

"Are you telling me that you got the wrong woman? A simple job and you bungled it."

Silas hid behind Helga who said, "It wasn't their fault, was it?"

"Sir," one of the men said, "we watched her get into her car with her friend. We had no way of knowing she would get out along the way. We could only track the car, not her."

Valdek turned his fury on him. "Gork will be beside himself with anger. He appointed me to get the job done."

For one brief second Silas saw that even this awful creature was afraid of Gork. Was being in the team really a safe option?

Silas buried his misgivings. He might be alright. "What about the Colonel, sir? What shall we do now he is married to her?

Valdek glowered at Silas. "They have the protection of the General these days. Get out all of you. We still have her energy signature and she *will* be stopped."

One by one they filed out of the room leaving Valdek in the darkened room.

***

Adam's house was quiet, very quiet. A few phone calls and a visit by the police had confirmed that Poppy and Joe were indeed the fatally injured victims. It was classed as a traffic accident due to their vehicle losing control.

Kate was inconsolable and walked around like a zombie whenever she left her room.

Feeling alone she cried, *"Why did you have to leave me, Poppy? Will you ever forgive me for bringing you here?"* Her shoulders shaking, she sobbed, her heart breaking. Across the room Jacob felt helpless as he watched his darling daughter but could do nothing to help as she rocked herself back and fore. She perched on a low stool by the fire in the sitting room and stared into the flames, thinking over the past. It was almost a year since she and Poppy had organised the lectures in Dorset. She couldn't know that it would almost be the last time that they would be together, sharing each other's thoughts and feelings, enjoying each other's company.

Kate looked across the room, not seeing anything, just staring with blank eyes, thinking of her dear friend. What was she doing now? Where was she now? *Why don't you speak to me Poppy?* she called, her heart anguished, beside herself with grief, and pain so bad she didn't think she could bear it. Tears streamed down her cheeks. She didn't think she could live through this. *Oh Poppy, oh Poppy, why have you left me? Why do you have to go now?* The tears kept coming and would not stop.

Jacob leaned back in his chair and closed his eyes. After a while Kate became aware of him in the room and remembered how fond of Poppy he was. She waited for him to speak while listening to the hiss of the burning wood in the fireplace. She realised he was gathering his thoughts. She waited through the silence until he opened his eyes. At last he reached his arms out to her and finally they cried together and rocked each other, comforting each other.

They were not the only ones grieving. Adam had been very fond of Poppy since the time he had met her. He remembered how welcoming she had been when they stayed at her home. She had been wonderful throughout all the trauma and excitement of visits to her door by men in black, to say nothing of Gork attempting to invade her home. He had been full of admiration of her handling of the situation when she was picked up by helicopter and accused of being a terrorist. Not many would deal with it all so well. She had been a friend indeed, and he missed her.

He also grieved for his driver, Joe. Joe had done nothing to deserve what happened to him. Adam determined to make sure his family would not suffer. Where would this all end? He was sure that the old General had nothing to do with the car accident. How did Silas and Helga figure in the attempt to kill Kate? He hadn't thought they could be so ruthless, but then how much did he really know.

There would be another attempt, of that he was sure. Also worrying was the thought that perhaps his position in the Shadow Government meetings might be compromised. He still had much work to do there. Perhaps bringing Kate to America was not such a good idea. Then he remembered that it was Master M's decision to do so, and he was usually right. In the meantime there were arrangements to be made to get Poppy's body back to England.

Adam went to find Kate, who stayed in her room too long and too often to be good for her. She needed to come alive again. He found her staring into space.

"Kate, listen to me," he said gently. "Are you listening to me? Are you listening to what I am saying? We have to make arrangements to get Poppy back to her home." In spite of himself his voice broke as he tried to continue.

"Yes she would like that." Kate's voice could hardly be heard. "The funeral should be there. It was her home after all. It is only right. I should never have taken her away." The tears flowed again."

Adam's heart was at breaking point seeing his loved one suffering so much. But he had to be strong for them all.

A day or two later he had it all in hand. They were to fly back together with Poppy in her coffin. He thanked the previous Colonel Fenshawe for the official status he had inherited from him. It really helped in smoothing out the technicalities of returning a body to its home country. One thing really troubled him. What were they to do with Poppy's beloved dogs? She had no living relatives, but perhaps she had made provisions for them in her will. He hoped with all his might that she had.

Would they ever find the real cause of the so-called accident? He doubted it, but one thing was clear, the old General had no hand in it. He had made it evidently clear that he had developed a fondness for them all. A sentimental streak had been opened in his heart.

To his great surprise, Francine declined to go back with them to UK. “I didn’t know her well,” she declared. “Not only that, but the General has invited me to stay for a while. How could I refuse him when he has been so kind?”

“That is mother all over,” commented Kate when she heard. He is welcome to her.”

***

Back on the Mothership Master M watched with the saddest of eyes the events of the last few days. “If only we could have prevented it,” he told Sechem and Jamère.

“But we mustn’t interfere, and they didn’t think to ask for help.”

Sechem tried to smile and failed. “They hadn’t foreseen the accident and so didn’t have the chance to ask for help. They were all so happy at the wedding.”

“Well, I did send the Legend of the Owl to Jacob, but he couldn’t have done anything anyway,” Jamère said.

Suddenly the colours around Master M flared brightly. “Look lads, I have a plan. As you know, Poppy was not very psychic, but now she is closer to us by not being physical. Being a beautiful soul she carries a high enough vibration to join us.”

Sechem gave a whoop. “Wow! She can become part of the team. We can work together.”

“If she wishes to,” said Master M. “It has to be her choice, not ours. At least we must give her a little time to adjust. She’ll be at the funeral of course.”

“Yes, it’s common for the deceased person to attend their own funeral. We laugh sometimes when we see the one who died holding a list of those attending, noting down what they are saying about them, and often, if it's a woman, noting what the people are wearing. It all depends on the time between death and the funeral. It is wise to allow at least three days after death for adjustment to the other world." Jamère said.

"Should we tell Kate?

"No, no, no. It has to be Poppy's decision alone, but you can sow the idea to her."

Jamère gave a little twirl. "Just an idea. Do you think Poppy's soul decided to go so she could do more good on the other side than when she was on Earth?"

Master M looked thoughtful.

"It's possible. Quite a few human souls make that decision when they feel they are not doing enough while alive. They sometimes feel they may be better at sowing seeds of ideas and thoughts into sleeping brains. It is often the more effective way. You yourself Sechem have done this with Kate, haven't you?"

"We'll just have to wait and see. We will all meet at the funeral. Agreed?"

***

They all stood around the grave, heads bowed, while the wind tossed the leaves at the tops of the trees planted here and there among the gravestones. The sun played a dance using the movement to dapple the ground and blind the eyes of the group standing there. They were a little knot of people isolated from the rest of the world by the railings that surrounded the cemetery.

Kate looked with sad eyes as the coffin was lowered. Was Poppy really in there? It seemed impossible that inside that indifferent wooden box lay someone she had touched and loved with all her might.

Some movement caught the corner of her eye. It came again. She turned her head to see four figures waving frantically at her through the patches of moving light, trying to catch her attention. It couldn't be, could it? She was inside that box. Yet there was Poppy standing beside Master M and the boys, happy and laughing. There was no mistake, it was her alright. Poppy put two fingers in her mouth and pulled a funny face causing Kate to smile and titter. This brought a sharp look from the vicar.

Kate wanted to tell Adam, but she knew she shouldn't and that he would not be able to understand right at that moment. Kate looked over to where four figures were standing. Then they waved, slowly turned and walked away into the shadows until she could see them no more.

She stayed where she was and tried to look sombre but inside her heart was singing with joy. Poppy hadn't left her after all.

***

Adam sat across the kitchen table from Kate and was puzzled by her smiling face. She ate her food with gusto and there was a light to her he had not seen since Poppy's death. She seemed to be happy and this he could not understand.

"Are you alright?" he asked.

"Darling Adam, I am perfectly alright. Let me tell you that Poppy has not left us at all."

Adam could not believe it. He frowned, worried about her reaction and denial of the fact that indeed Poppy was gone in the cruellest way. It had been too much for her to accept. He got up from the table and went to put his arms round her. "Darling, . . . "

Kate stopped him. "Let me explain, dear Adam. She was there at the funeral. I saw her clearly. She was with Sechem, Jamère and Master M. They were together. Can you believe that?"

Adam blinked. It was possible of course. He understood now. He watched Kate smiling to herself. She knew that life went on, for hadn't she been to the *'other side'* herself and played with unborn children? He already accepted that communication is possible with those who had left the physical body. Sechem was proof of that, for he too had once been on Earth, as she was now. All she needed to do now was to go into her 'altered state' and she could be with Poppy once more. Knowing Kate, he knew she would do that as soon as she was alone.

***

A day or two later a sombre group waited around the highly polished table in the solicitor's office. No one spoke as they took their seats. Jacob seemed to be ridiculously focused on the loud tick tock of a clock on a shelf near the door. He wanted to throw something at it, anything to break the tension. Adam was surprised and pleased to see a smile on Kate's face and wondered at it. Had she already made contact with Poppy?

At last the solicitor walked in carrying a file. He sat and acknowledged them with a brief nod. He threw a serious look at all the faces before him.

"I am sure you are aware that Poppy Mills was well respected in the community and gave much of her time to helping others. She will be missed by all. As you may know she had no living relatives. He paused and read out a long list of donations to various charities."

I didn't know she had so many interests," Jacob whispered to his daughter.

"Be quiet, Dad. He is not finished."

The solicitor looked up and focused his attention on Kate. "I leave the rest of my entire estate to my beloved friend Kate Greene on the proviso that her father Jacob Greene resides indefinitely on my property and takes care of my dogs for as long as they shall live."

Jacob listened in stunned silence. He began to weep and fumbled for a tissue. Kate handed one to him and put her arms around him.

"There, there Dad. Don't take on so. This is marvellous and you loved it there when we visited, didn't you?"

Adam moved over to Jacob and shook his hand vigorously. "Congratulations Jacob. You are exactly the right man for the job. Poppy knew what she was doing alright."

At the mention of Poppy tears welled up again in Jacob's eyes and threatened to spill over.

"Dad, the solicitor has finished now, but you will need to see him again to finalise details. Adam and I will stay in England until it is all sorted. Then we will have our honeymoon."

***

Kate went to bed with many questions buzzing round in her head. Was everything set to happen? Was Poppy's death part of the plan or do we all make our own plan as we go? She fell asleep thinking about it.

That night Kate had another journey and as before it was a conversation with *'the voice'*.

My stairs are wooden steps, slats of wood. Unusual and not like normal stairs at all. I'm trying to get my head round this. I have to go on each slat and not skip any, since they are so shallow, I would be tempted to take two at a time. I must not skip any single one, but go on each tread.

"This is true for each of you as go through life. You cannot skip any part of it through wishful thinking or wanting to change the route. If you wish to finish your journey correctly you must tread on each slat that is presented to you. You might stay on one slat awhile and explore the feelings, the emotions and decisions that come to your eyes, or you may move on swiftly. There is no skipping, no dancing around it, however you may feel"

"The slats represent what exactly?" Kate asks.

"Each slat represents a part of your life, a period in your life. It may be long, or it may be short. These are steps on your way to greater understanding."

"OK, I've got that. I mustn't skip anything. I am looking for information. Can you help me there?"

"Each step will give you meaning and information. To give it to you in advance would be foolish, for you must deal with whatever is presented as it comes."

"That I can understand."

"You are now thinking, does this relate to teaching others? It is the same thing. Each step is important to everybody, no matter what is happening in every part of your world. There are still experiences that must be gone through in order to gain fuller understanding."

"Does this mean we can't change anything?"

"It is not a question of changing, it is a question of understanding and seeing things in a different light so that you may deal with it in that light."

"Are we totally alone in this?"

"No, you will always have guidance, depending on whether you wish to have guidance or whether you wish to do it all by yourself."

"Am I going to pass this on?"

"Yes, it is important that everything we give you is presented for the soul's journey, even if it does not seem to be of benefit. In fact more is gained by not feeling comfortable for you will learnt how to deal with the difficult things as well as the easy things."

Kate woke, thought about what she had been given and soon fell asleep again. Another dream soon presented itself.

This time I go up on wide carpeted stairs. I get to a landing which branches off on both sides. I can go either side as they meet again on another landing. Going up another level I am told. I hear Gustav Holtz's Saturn, of the Planet Suite.

"All of the solar system is playing harmonics to assist Earth. All are affected, some will hear, some will not, some will see and feel, yet others will not. A division again. DNA changes for all who are affected by the harmonics."

Kate woke with even more questions in her mind. Were they ever going to let her sleep properly? Then she remembered that Sechem had told her that if she was not meditating for information, he would give it to her in her dreams. What she did with it was up to her.

Kate accepted that if she wished to have a good night's sleep she should meditate more often.

CHAPTER FOURTEEN

INFORMATION FLOWING

The way forward. Look for the way forward. If you are looking you will see it. It is evident and not at all hidden. Seek out the Wisdoms of the Ages which lie within you. If you look far enough, you will also see far into the future time. All is the same, no past, no present and no future separation. It is all together in you.

Erasmus

Adam was restless. He felt he was not doing his job at discovering vital information of the Shadow Government's plans to give to the Spiritual Galactic Command. After all this was why he had been asked to take over the body of Colonel Adam Fenshawe who wanted out of his life. Adam wondered what the poor man was doing now that he was released from an insufferable existence. Probably enjoying himself, Adam reflected. The best part of the exchange was meeting Kate, falling in love and marrying her. It couldn't get any better than that. However it was time to get moving and do his job.

He found Kate in the garden doing a little weeding. Her father was going to need some help keeping the grounds in order.

"Kate? Kate, are you busy? I need to ask you something." She looked up, wiping some dirt off her face. He loved her so much. "I wonder how you feel about having some more of your journeys. I know you have had a lot to deal with recently, but I think it is important not to let your gift go. It was given to you for a purpose."

Kate looked up from her weeding and smiled. It was the answer to her question after her dream. It made everything clear. "Darling, I absolutely agree. How about this evening, and Dad can join us? It will be like old times. Perhaps Sechem or Jamère will appear too."

***

That evening the light was going and all was peaceful outside. The dogs had settled for the night after Jacob had taken them for their walk. He was more than ready to sit and relax. He hoped he wouldn't fall asleep as he so often did. His daughter would soon be returning to America with Adam and this could be the last time they worked together. He wanted to make the most of it.

Chairs were in place and phones switched off. Kate sat comfortably in her chair as she went down into herself. The two men watched as she began to fade.

"Speak to us," said Jacob.

She began: My stairs are very shallow, easy gradation down making it effortless for me. I am going somewhere very deep. Suddenly I see there are walls on either side. I didn't expect this. The steps are encased by the walls, but there is no indication of where I am going. The walls are of rough stone or cement. I keep moving. There are a few sounds coming in and I can *feel* them coming in. I thank them but they seem to be waiting.

I ask, "Will I have to speak before you come in? That seems to be the key. You pick up on my sound frequency. The effect of sound. I am aware that you are here. I am looking for something important to share."

At last I get to something. It is very dark and the path leads into a tunnel. I can still see because there is just enough light to see, and they know I must see. I must not go blindfold to anything here. I go forward. The ground is very rough. I don't think anyone has been this way before or it would have been smooth. This is untrodden territory.

"OK! So show me. Show me where I must go, please."

In front there is a green wall, a curtain. I don't know what to call it. I know from experience that I must go through this.

"It is a screen, screening from those who do not understand."

"So, why should it be screened?"

"Because they cannot cope with what is behind the screen."

"Am I allowed to go through?"

"You are to help them adjust to reality."

I walk forward, through it. I am no longer myself; I am another being, tall, thin. But I still have a female feel about me. I think this is another part of me. As I walk through, the scene is of desolation and destruction.

"It is how parts of your planet are becoming as a result of warfare. People are on the move, away from the war zones."

"I know that already." I tell them.

"These places that were homes have become desolate. Nobody there. The land was rich in all that it had before, but the people have fled, hoping to find something more. As warfare increases, they take with them their own inability to manage affairs. They simply take these troubles with them. And so the effect of war spreads, even without bombs and killing. This must change if you are to save your planet. For people in these situations do not, will not ever have the ability or capacity to make the changes themselves, and so they spread and spread the trouble.

"However, within these mass evacuations, mass exodus there are bright souls, new souls, special envoys sent from spirit to assist. All is not as dire as you might think. We are doing all we can in this respect. Warfare must stop. War is not only killing people, it is destroying the land and bringing it to destruction. This must not spread like a cancer.

"After a period of time, when the desolate areas, by that we mean devoid of humans, then nature will take over once more and the creatures of the land will return. Then you will find people beginning to return. It all takes time. It is so unfortunate that this is the way your years have become. There will be light in these war-torn areas again, given time. Time is the important factor here. We know it will regrow, be reborn and people will continue to produce children who are wiser than they.

"Your real problem is those who wish to control the world. That is where the source of all this is."

"Why cannot we do something about those people who are ruining the planet?" I ask.

"We will not allow the planet itself to be destroyed. Each individual upon the planet is responsible, as always for his or her interaction, decisions and growth. That must be at all times. You have another question? Please put it."

"What is happening to human beings, children, adults who suddenly disappear, vanish? What is happening to them? Where are they?"

"As you are aware there are many causes, not just one. Seeing it from our standpoint some of those who vanish are being kept clear of destruction. They are being taken to safe zones off planet. They will continue to be nurtured, to exist as human beings. Within this plan there are several bi- purposes that will - - - *long pause as if thinking.*

"There are others who disappear, who are indeed taken by your own people for their own dire purposes, and not out of consideration for the humans they take. This too is true. As you are already aware of the law of karma, those who do these deeds will receive the same treatment in their own soul journey. That too will be regrettable. That is another law that cannot be shaken."

At this point Sechem arrived in the room, shaking his head. "This won't do, whoever you are. This is no comfort to those who have lost loved ones in this way."

The voice continued through Kate. "That law will never be broken. There is nothing we can do to change that. You did ask for information and that is what we are giving."

Sechem was not satisfied. He turned his attention on Kate. "Kate, ask to be shown another scenario, if you will please."

"I'll do my best," she said.

They all waited in silence broken only by the crackle and sparks of the wood burning in the fireplace. Time passed. All of a sudden Kate began again in a lighter voice.

"It is not easy you know jumping from one world to another. You ought to try it some time.

"I have crystal stairs this time, white and almost liquid, like clear ice. I can see through them. There doesn't seem to be a side to them as the stairs stretch both sides as far as the eye can see. I am not slipping, and it is warm to the feet, so it can't really be ice. Glass? It must be glass. It is a very gentle slope down.

"You don't need to go deep because you are already deep." Sechem told her.

"Oh, that's good. I've got to keep going." It feels as if I am not alone. In fact there are, I am going to call them souls going in both directions. Some going up and some going down. This is not what I expected. "Where is this taking me?"

"You are going into the depths of knowledge. Some have been before and then return to put what they have learnt into practice. That is what you are doing, going into the depths of knowledge, grasping what you can understand, and then bringing it back with further experiences, and spreading the knowledge that you gain."

"That's lovely but I must know what the knowledge is."

I have just reached the bottom and all I can see are little lights dancing around. The lights are intelligences and they keep bobbing up and down, excited. They do not appear to have a form attached to them. As I move forward they part the way for me. They move freely. All these lights are intelligences, sparks of knowing. I need to know what they are knowing otherwise these are just words and not information.

"Hmm! The knowing comes from within, not from without."

I have a picture of hands coming from all directions, joining hands and doing it in unison.

"We all understand each other, and we all accept each other's variance, and still hold hands in love. There you will have the heaven you are looking for."

"This seems to be unattainable in this world."

"Maybe, but if you hold that vision of these souls, not just human beings, we are speaking of all sentient beings. Sentient beings who will accept everyone for what they are, without trying to change them to their own way of thinking. Then there will be peace, when each does not try to outdo the other, when each puts out a helping hand to another."

"I am thinking as I am getting this, we DO know this already, but how can we put it into practice? How can we help others to see this and act upon it? That is the difficulty."

"You must at least try to begin to see it happening in individuals in your head. If you can't visualise it, how on Earth can it happen? So, visualise it. that is a start. It must start with you, as it must start with each sentient being."

"Look Adam," Jacob said, "She is coming back. Do you ever think we will have the peace she spoke of, in this world?"

"I truly hope so," Adam replied as Kate resumed her form.

CHAPTER FIFTEEN

UNIVERSAL KNOWLEDGE AND INTELLIGENCE

Shifting sands, shifting sands. Smooth movement of land, vast land. Nothing is recognisable, nothing is left of former times. Move on, move on. The new is fresh, the new is welcoming you. Forget the past, forget the now. Look ahead. It is almost here. Can't you see it coming? Do not be caught unawares. Do not waste time. Get your mind settled in peace and readiness. The change is for you. You will do this with no company alongside except me. I am Ra, the greatest of all. Come with me. Be with me on my beam of life and you will know all.

Jacob was well pleased that Kate had brought through important information whether it was accepted or not. He went to sleep contented and relieved that he hadn't after all fallen asleep. Maybe he too would now receive as he once did. He no long had pressure on him now that Adam would take care of Kate. He drifted off into a deep dream in which he heard,

"I am the Spirit of the Earth. The spirit of the ground on which you stand and the produce that enables you to survive. I am the spirit of the Earth that you rest upon and depend upon. I am the mountains and the seas, the forests, and the streams. I am the lakes and the hills and all those things which make up this Earth. I am the strength that holds this together. I am the father of the mother Earth, the component that supports and nourishes. The one that makes the decisions as to how we may best survive together. I am the one who listens to all the doings of man and the thoughts that affect me. I thank you for your goodly thoughts. I thank you for all the attention that you give me. I am stronger than all of you and will survive.

"I am soon to change. I am soon to make some adjustments, for I too am evolving. I too will make alterations on the face of my being. The reality that you see, feel and touch will undergo a reshaping. The nourishment that I provide will still be there, but different. I am frequently called Mother Earth, but this mother has the male element also and not one in favour of the other, but in equal parts. I am a consciousness speaking to you.

"I observe all things that take place upon the surface of my being, in much the same way as your soul and your vibration absorbs the vibration of others around you and from the air and form the spirits.

"I absorb into my being that which is on the surface. All illnesses, all thoughts, all goodness, and by so doing these elements are cleansed, for they pass through me."

Jacob asked of the spirit, "Do trees purify thought forms, negative thought forms, as happens with the Cosmos?"

"All things that exist upon me, that are living and act in harmony with the elements of nature that is on my being, act as a cleansing, a purification. It is part of the balancing of nature. This can destroy or it can purify. Much depends on the balancing effect. We have no control over the deeds of man, but we have a purifying effect on their thoughts and their nature.

"We are aware of the vibrational content of all things that are upon the surface, that are within us also. All things. The rumbling of the earthquake and the fire of the volcano is part of us. It is part of the balancing of nature that is us also. We say 'us' for we are both male and female working together in total harmony."

Jacob woke with a start before he had a chance to ask any more questions.

***

Next morning he could hardly wait to tell Adam and Kate what he had received in his sleep. He was so excited. He would be able to do his work wherever he was, as long as he had questions in his mind that he wanted answers to. He had not lost his previous training as a psychic after all.

Adam and Kate listened over breakfast and were thrilled to hear what he had to say.

Jacob thought hard before speaking again. He didn't want to give them too much to think about when they had already gone through so much. But he could not hold back his enthusiasm.

"You will be leaving very soon for your honeymoon and I don't want to delay or spoil that. Helga and Silas seem to have gone to ground so I don't think we have to worry too much about them."

Adam and Kate looked at each other and wondered what was coming next. "Yes, Dad? So?"

"Do you think we could fill the time you have left here with me in connecting with our spirit friends before you leave? It is a lot to ask, but I feel it is important somehow. What do you think?"

Adam smiled. "It is just what we were going to suggest, Jacob. We could start tonight. Perhaps too we could all work together, make a journey together. We have never tried that before. What can we lose?"

They got all their various jobs around the property done in record time. Kate felt that Poppy would be pleased with their efforts. Both Jacob and Adam were convinced that they had seen the last of Helga and Silas. The combined assistance from Sechem, Jamère and Master M had probably been too much for them and saw them dispensed with by Valdek and the team as being useless. They had no further role to play.

Feeling energised they sat together in the quiet, and after saying a prayer they went inwards to meditate and waited.

Kate opened up, speaking first as usual.

"I see myself as an energy form, all different colours. I am moving my way down on what appears to be a knotted rope. I need to count the knots. As I count I go deeper and am going very deep into the bowels of the Earth. As an energy form I am entering where a physical form cannot go. As an energy I can go anywhere. I can be anything. So I go down, I don't even feel I'm passing through anything physical. Oh I see. It is the energy of the Earth that I am entering, in the same way that I am an energy form, so is the Earth. It does not need to be physical."

"That is just what she did when she entered the tea trolley" said Adam.

I ask, "As I travel, does the Earth… is it conscious of itself in the way I am conscious of me?"

"Of course it's conscious of itself. The Earth is aware of every part of itself as are you when you are physical. You are aware of anything that touches upon you: so it is with the Earth. The Earth is fully aware of the damage that is being done by other intelligent forms. You are all intelligent forms, all of you, deciding what to do or what not to do. The whole thing is driven by decision and action so that there might be a reaction."

"I am a bit lost here, I am still going down the rope and I am used to seeing something physical, and not being energy."

"The energy affects every single thing, and that includes you as you go down into us. We say ***us*** because we are not single as you might have imagined. The planet Earth is a multiple as are you. As multiple intelligences you are aware of the other multiples of you, as the Earth is aware of the multiples of itself."

"This is all getting a bit deep for me (excuse the pun)."

"But you see, we can communicate, can we not, through intelligence. You are, as you have been told, an interpreter of the intelligence we put into words so that you may pass it on. There is no other way for us to communicate with those who are not aware of the intelligence."

"It is so very hard. How can I explain this?"

"We, as multiple Earths will continue to exist, as you as a multiple will continue to exist. We, as the Earth in connecting as a physical form is the one to be conscious of, as the you, as the being you have become in your multiple will always be aware of what is happening to you."

"How can all this knowledge help the Earth and its peoples to move in the correct direction?"

"What is correct? What is correct for one is deemed incorrect for another."

"That is certainly truc." I say. "Is it correct that the Earth that you are connecting with now be damaged in some way?"

"I would say no, it is not correct."

"But that is from your perspective."

"Surely, you as that Earth have the right to an opinion on this." I point out.

"But you see. We are multiples. We will not cease to exist, and we have choices and we will, according to what is interacting with us, negative or positive, we will react and interact accordingly to our interests."

"Your own interests are your own concern. In a roundabout way you are saying what we already know. It doesn't help us make decisions."

"You must make your own decisions. We cannot influence you in any way. Your existence must be of your own creation, as it is for each intelligence."

"It is all getting a bit hard to understand."

"It will be easy if you give it some thought. As a non-physicality we do not wish to disturb your energy form too much. You are not ready to become only an intelligence, not yet."

Kate felt the pressure. "I don't think I can hold it anymore. Could one of you take over please? Remember, form your intention and it will happen."

"Sechem please help," said Adam. "This is new for us. We need you."

The TV set in the corner sprang into life. The familiar buzzing and zigzag appeared on the screen.

"Oh Sechem, can't you just arrive like everybody else?" Jacob said.

"I am not everybody else." Sechem giggled as he said this. It was clear he was enjoying the new arrangement. "Which one shall it be?" He looked at the men, pondered and then waved an arm over Jacob. Jacob's head fell forward and he began to speak. "Oh, that was easy," exclaimed Sechem.

Jacob's voice was gruff. "I'm getting shafts off the sun, like sunlight beams. They are very precise and are coming from a global sun. Global Sun?

"Yes, the sun that is your own personal sun for Earth. You must call that Global Sun, surely? It is for your solar system. The beams that are sent out cover the entire solar system and each beam that is *now* being sent has been intelligently designed to produce a specific outcome. As in the past some of the outpourings of the sun have been deflected away from the Earth, so that it did not adversely affect it. Yet other rays have not been deflected. The rays, the beams that are being sent now are not being deflected but are monitored. Some elements will touch the Earth and change the Earth in ways that cannot be undone."

"What is this intelligence that is making these arrangements?"

"The intelligence comes from the Universal Galactic Command. They are able to decide what is required for any particular planet anywhere in the universe we control. We are the intelligence of your universe, and so you might say we are able to manipulate for benefit or otherwise any particular planet, not just in your solar system, but any particular planet in any system within your universe.

"This is different to being affected just by your sun, it expands beyond that. It exists beyond your Milky Way, and all the other Earth-like planets and all the other sun systems. We from our intelligence can to a certain extent direct the physical future of others. We laugh when we see or hear of the, what shall we say, the actions of those, of what you call the 'Shadow Government'. They are insignificant in comparison to what we can do. You may feel they are having an effect on your weather and climate when in fact *we* have the greater control, not they.

"There is much more to be said on this, but we will keep that for another time. This is of enormous interest to those who believe in the larger scheme of things. It will take their minds way beyond their own personal considerations on the Earth. We are glad to have made contact. We will make contact again very soon."

"Look," Adam cried, "Kate may be disappearing again. We must pay attention."

Jacob remained in a deep state, carefully controlled by Sechem.

Kate said, "While making a connection I was urged to speak ET language. Another different one. I had intended to make connection with a cosmic force. After I'd made my connection, which I now feel strongly, I am placed in a corridor, a clean tidy corridor, glass windows along both sides. It could be a corridor anywhere, in a hospital or office. It is very efficient and long. As I walk along, I see each office door and window has been allocated a task. Kate muttered something unintelligible then began again in a clear voice.

"Nobody can do everything all at once. There is always allocation to tasks and a unit behind that allocation. It is teamwork, for one person alone cannot do it all. That you must remember. In order for you to carry out your task you need to decide what it is that holds most of your attention. Then you will be directed to the correct, shall we say, office? The correct team will work alongside you in that endeavour. You need not think that you are doing it alone. Each endeavour is accompanied by those who have the same interests at heart. This does not mean that other concerns are not of interest, simply that it is beneficial to focus more closely on the one that has your heart. It does not mean that you do not care about the others. Simply, as we have said, focus on one and work with that team. Have we made that clear?"

"It has, but I would still like guidance. What is the most important focus for me?"

"For this present time in your incarnation, your focus should be getting the information we pass to you out to the general public. That much we feel you already know."

"So, this involves making sure I connect with the team for the information."

"No, that is not quite correct. You focus on getting the information by asking questions during contact and enquiring, the team then will assist you in getting it out. Do you see the difference?"

"Yes, I see the difference. So, to get the information the question is, what part of information is the most important? There is information of all kinds."

"We are guiding you even more now into information on the Laws of the Universe and the way it is run. We know you are not a scientist, but there are levels of information that we can give you in simple terms so that you can then present them in layman terms. Then everyone will understand without being of scientific mind."

"That will suit me beautifully. Re the information, how can I get this? How will it be given to me, or to anyone?"

"As always it will be given through your mind in meditation."

"Mmm! That does give me a little problem."

"Just follow your normal pattern. We will provide the scenes that will make it clear. You are also being guided to see possible futures. *This* is important, to see the possible futures so that choices can be made. We are talking about predictions now. We talk about possibilities not set in cast iron, but what could happen if things in the minds of others are not brought to attention."

What follows is the talking. This is important because when you write you learn things you didn't know before, and you must have it clear in your head if you are going to speak on these things."

"That makes sense. Do I have one team for both or is there a team for each? Speaking and writing."

"As we have said, one leads to the other."

"Will you give me something now, while I am in contact with you? You did tell me to ask if I want to know."

"She is cheeky," said Sechem, as he listened.

Kate had her request answered and said, "I see a whole city laid out. But it is silent, nothing is happening in that city. It is like looking at the past. Only this is not the past that I am seeing. It is so quiet, no smoke anywhere, nothing, nothing, it is dead. No sound of traffic, no lights, no general hum that one gets with the city. Nothing. Why, why, is there no sign of life?"

"This is the future that you are seeing, for one portion of land. This is the future that you are seeing."

"Where have the people gone?"

"Some are still around, but not there. They have vacated themselves elsewhere. Some were too late, for they did not believe."

"What about other areas?"

"It is a pattern which is repeated elsewhere. It is a pattern in many parts of your globe."

"Why am I seeing it? I want to know why. Why are you showing it to me?"

"You can do something about this. You can alert men's minds. You can prepare them; give them serenity before the event so that serenity carries them through. Give them the connection with their own souls, for this is what will carry them through. You can tell them this doesn't have to be."

"I'll do my best." Kate's voice was so quiet now that the men hardly heard her.

"She is tiring. It has been too much," Sechem said. "Come back now, Kate."

Adam watched Kate, who gradually came back to her form, but who remained in a deep state alongside her father.

"What about me, Sechem? Am I not going to receive anything of value?"

Sechem understood Adam's need to be included. "Well if I watch over you all I suppose it could be arranged," he said. "This is not usual, you understand that, don't you?"

Adam nodded vigorously. Maybe the experience he had before was a one off too. Sechem waved his arm over him and Adam lost himself in the new gift and started to speak.

"My stairs are slippery and shiny. I need to hold on to the bannisters to make sure I don't fall. I am only just keeping my feet. It is as if I am on ice and I haven't any skating boots, just my normal shoes which have no grip. I go down anyway knowing that if I let go of the banisters I will fall. As I go further down it is getting warmer and the ice is melting. It is watery now. I have ground covered in water. It is getting a lot warmer now and steam is coming off the water. I step off the last step onto rocky, gritty ground, gravelly, that's the word.

"As I look around and ask to be shown something, I see two beings come forward and each takes a hand and guides me forward.

They have got my arms, so I feel good and safe. They are large beings, with strong and muscular bodies. They are clothed, but I can see they are brawny. They have strength and are taking me somewhere.

"Where are you taking me?"

"We are taking you to meet your demons."

"I didn't know I had any demons."

"We are taking you to show you that if you believe you have demons, then you have. If you don't believe you have then you don't have."

"So why this show? Why?"

"You will discover if you have demons or not. We are still taking you somewhere."

We seem to be going into a glade. Fresh bright green, trees, fresh grass. It is beautiful and there is loveliness here – no demons – no demons. So why am I told to face my demons? Where are they? The two beings turn me to the side, drop my arms and say,

"Go into the bushes alone."

I have done this so many times, so I walk into the bushes and they seem to part as I go through.

"What is this all about?"

"You are going into new pastures. Your life ahead is going to take a different turn, one that you cannot see ahead so that you cannot plan. It will occur and you will face whatever it is as it occurs."

"OK. I have always done that."

"Yes, but you have no idea what this is. As yet you have no idea where this will be. It will take you into different realities of your life on Earth."

"I still don't understand this but am happy if they have a good effect."

"Oh, they will have an effect alright. Please be assured of that."

"It seems to be taking a heck of a long time."

"Things will happen at the right time as always."

I have a picture of men tearing up papers and substituting others in their place. I can't quite work that one out.

"The papers are documents relating to scientific research. Figures, calculations and formulae long established will be replaced. A new thinking, a new direction of endeavour is required. The old conditioning will be swept aside. Restructure, there is to be restructure *(of energies?)*"

"Restructure of both on a material and physical level. Genetically speaking there is to be re-structure, one might say rapid evolution. Yes, indeed there will be changes which you cannot imagine."

I ask for a picture. It sounds absolutely crazy. It's a picture of people in the air without any visible means of support.

"It is a demonstration of ability to defy gravity, anti-gravity you might say. It is not necessary to escape the pull of your earth to experience this and to utilise this in many ways for transport and other objectives useful to mankind. It has in fact been done before; this has been achieved in your past but was misused. It will be so again."

Sechem waved his arm over him and Adam returned at once, fresh and clear headed.

"Wow! That was intriguing. I don't know whether to be happy or worried about all that. It felt very personal and for me alone, not for anyone else. Wait till I tell Kate. Oh, she is still under I see.

"Jacob is beginning to come back to us," Sechem said. "He will watch the next bit that she will bring though."

"Oh, so you already know what she is going to say?" Adam was amazed.

"Remember dear friend I am a Time Traveller and past, present and future are all connected. We have told you that."

Where Kate was sitting they saw a blue wave of energy pass through her. Her form shivered, and then she sat bolt upright. They all thought she was going to stand and walk about. But instead she raised both arms as if giving a speech. A strong vibrant male voice came from her open mouth.

"All is in order. You are breaking new ground. The ground of the undisclosed. This is important, for that which was not known is to be known and will surprise many. There will be those who do not understand, and those who already know, but who hold it within their hearts. So whatever you discover you must put it out for others to make their own decisions whether to receive or reject. All is in order, despite what many may say. There will be upset, there will be calm and acknowledgement, but what is to be is for the best of the whole of the Human Race. Do not doubt it, even in moments when you feel doubt strongly. Remind yourself that all is in order."

Adam breathed a sigh of relief. "All is in order then, eh? I hope so." He noticed that Kate was starting to flop over. "Fetch her out Sechem, I think she has done enough."

Sechem waved his arms over all of them. "Not a bad evening, was it? Are you happy now?"

Jacob stretched and got up. "I think we all need to celebrate a successful group session. How about some champagne?"

Kate was wide awake now and sat up straight at that. "Now, Dad. In moderation please. You know how you get once a bottle is opened."

"I am a changed man, don't forget. I have responsibilities now. Don't worry about me." He went to the cabinet and got out the glasses and bottles. "One for you Sechem?"

Sechem waved him away, laughing. "You know I can't drink Jacob. Well done all."

Next moment he was not there.

***

Next morning, nursing a headache, Jacob took the dogs out for their usual walk. He watched Poppy's favourite dog Boris prancing around. The large wolfhound suddenly stopped, became still and seemed to be staring at something Jacob could not see.

"I know, old boy. She is still here, isn't she?" He knew that many animals could see even from the spirit world, those they loved on Earth. He felt comforted.

"I'll look after them, and Kate," he called out promising Poppy and hoped she had heard him.

There had been no further interference from Silas and Helga. From what Adam had been able to discover, they had both joined what they called 'The Team'. Good luck to them, he said to himself as he went indoors to settled down and make a cup of tea, with biscuits of course.

CHAPTER SIXTEEN

FRESH ORDERS

Somewhere on some planet, sometime and somehow
Your life will reflect your thoughts of your now.
My law in unerring, no blood can atone,
the structure you built, you will live in, alone.
From cycle to cycle, through time and through space,
your lives with your longings will ever keep pace.
All that you ask for, and all you desire
must come at your bidding as flame out of fire.
From the Emerald Tablets

Silas didn't know whether to be pleased or disappointed at the news that came on official letter heading and read:
You are being transferred to our headquarters in Dulce on the New Mexico Colorado border.

First of all he had no idea there was a headquarters there. What was he to do at that place? The pleasing part was that he was now part of The Team and with that came power. It would not be so bad after all. He smiled to himself. He had arrived. He packed his belongings and set off for his flight.

A uniformed man met him on arrival and led him to a blacked-out car. He tried to have a conversation with the driver and failed. The journey was long and tiring through the Jicarilla Apache Reservation near Mount Archuleta. An hour later the car stopped, and another uniformed man escorted him to a small building hidden away behind a wooden fence. Was this it? Silas's face dropped in dismay. This surely could not be any kind of headquarters. Then he remembered how dismal and tucked away was the building for surveillance in DC. His heart lifted again.

There were no security pads or screenings that he could see. On knocking on the door someone inside said, 'Come in'.

He opened the door cautiously. Who would be there to greet him now he considered he was one of The Team? When he saw who it was he almost ran back out in shock. Standing proudly behind a desk was Helga.

She leaned forward to shake his hand. "Hello Silas. We meet again. It seems we are to work together. I have been here a week now and it is not bad at all. Lots to do so I hope you are up to it, this time."

Silas was lost for words. His mind could not function after the shock of seeing her there. He shook her hand and looked around for a chair for his shaky legs.

It took Silas a moment or two before he could trust himself to speak. When he did it came out as a squeak. "How, how did you manage to get here? What are we going to be working on? I have not been told anything, just to report here."

He looked at her pompous expression and wished he could throttle her. Were they going to be on equal terms? "Have they told you anything?" he asked.

Helga looked at him with disdain. "As I said, there is a lot to do."

"Don't tell me we are still going to run around after those two troublemakers Kate and Jacob?" Silas said and hoped it was not the case. He had had enough. And what about his joining the team?

Helga pointed to a small desk on the other side of the room. "That is where you will sit," she said. "We are all part of the team, but you will operate under my orders."

Silas groaned aloud causing Helga to look up sharply. "What did you say?"

He wished he was anywhere but here near her, but what could he do now?

"Our first task has been given not too far away from here. It should be easy enough and even you couldn't bungle it. We have our orders from Gork and when we have accomplished our task I can follow through on eliminating Kate. You needn't concern yourself any longer on that score."

"Good luck with that," Silas sneered. "I understand that Gork is on his own now and without protection from the Confederation, so go easy on obeying his every order," was all he could think of saying.

***

The task was to be carried out in a private hall not far from Dulce airport. Helga and Silas's job was to arrange and engage in a military operation under the Shadow Government's space force and report back.

In the nearby town regular meetings were held in a private hall to discuss strange sightings in the sky. A little group of people gathered together whose mission it was to provide a meeting ground for people and groups of opposing and often controversial views, in the hope that in working together they could further overall knowledge in these areas and promote scientific research. Their ultimate goal was to help humankind have a better understanding of the overall nature of unusual personal experiences and to support those who have them. Such experiences may include close encounters with non-human entities, and/or UFO activity. None of them knew they were all about to have a real experience they would never forget.

The latest meeting was already underway, and several people were standing around talking and putting their points of view over.

Nobody there noticed twelve-year-old Jamie hiding nearby. He was looking at a flat metal plate with buttons on it that had not been there previously. He was puzzled. He was sure it hadn't been there before, and he had visited this hall many times. He knew every inch of it. Curiosity got the better of him and he pressed one button that stood out from the rest of the others.

As he did so all bedlam broke loose. Jamie scurried from the scene as fast as his legs would go. He hadn't intended any of this to happen. How was he to know the consequences of that one little push. There were no warning labels. He was not to blame.

Looking back into the room he was astounded to see a wave of red wash over everything and everyone there. They looked as if they were frozen in time, unable to move. From doors on all sides teams of black uniformed men burst in waving guns and shouting.

"Everyone stay absolutely still!"

That's daft, thought Jamie. They couldn't move even if they wanted to. What was that red stuff? He hid behind a pillar and watched, afraid to stay, but unwilling to leave.

The uniformed men moved quickly and surrounded those unfortunate to be caught. They herded them into a tight group and began to move them out of the door. The boy dared not follow. What should he do now? He waited until the room was empty and the red had cleared. Cautiously and with a beating heart he moved to the nearest door and looked out to see where they had gone. There was nothing to see at first, but then he became aware of a humming noise overhead. Looking up he was just in time to see it before it shot off clear up into the sky.

Jamie's legs buckled under him and he slumped to the floor. What should he do? Should he report what he had seen, and if he did who would believe him anyway?

***

On level four below the surface, men stood waiting for a report on the exercise. The giant creature known as Valdek headed the group.

"Were you seen?" he barked.

The small group of military men shuffled their feet uncomfortably.

"We are not sure," one ventured.

"Not sure? There must be no mistakes in this." Valdek swung round to face them.

A slick officer festooned with medals raised his voice. "The local police had a report from a young boy about a group of people being taken out of the room and disappearing into the sky," he said. "But the police didn't believe his story."

"What was anyone from outside doing in that area?" the creature thundered. He turned his attention of Helga And Silas. "You were supposed to arrange this. Someone will pay for this."

Not a soul doubted that for a moment. An overweight man coughed politely. "I believe the young boy is the son of one of the cleaners. He got curious about the regular meetings and sneaked in when no one was looking."

"Unbelievable! With all the security checks we make, this is not to be allowed."

Silas and Helga kept their eyes lowered. What was coming next? They didn't have to wait long.

Valdek looked them up and down. "You two will stay below on level seven until I decide otherwise. Your things will be brought to you here.

CHAPTER SEVENTEEN

FINAL DECISION

Joy is in the air for there are changes afoot. There is great excitement and anticipation over the events, which have been in the planning for so very long. We are awaiting the birth of a new child, the coming of the new race of man. What joy! What wonder! What thanksgiving is present in all the Celestial Hosts over this new dawning of mankind. Be forever grateful for being present at this time.

Elsewhere way above Earth, Sechem, Jamère and Master M held a little celebration.

"Well that's settled now. No more trouble from those two at last. We can breathe easy. Well done my friends," Master M clapped them both on the back. Just one more job and then we can relax.

The Great Hall on the Mothership was buzzing. It seemed that all the lights in the Universe had been turned on. The Big Decision was about to be announced. The leaders of the Spiritual Galactic Confederation were soon to arrive. Not needing vehicles or any physical form it was understood that in order to be seen and understood by many races at all dimensional levels, as a concession they would take visual form at this unusual gathering. This arrangement could only be held for a limited time.

A hush fell over the assembly as gentle music heralded their arrival in the Great Hall. Many holographic forms took their places and appeared to hover.

"It's all an illusion," whispered Master M to Sechem and Jamère, sitting alongside a glowing figure of Poppy.

"I know," she whispered back with a huge smile. Nothing would or could go wrong while the Great Ones were overseeing Earth. Contented she leant back in her seat. *None of this is physically real* she told herself.

The following words were sent telepathically to all and were heard and understood by each race attending this great moment. They knew of only five other times when it had been necessary for the Human Race to be discussed in this way. Many remembered those occasions very well, but for Master M this was a first. He listened intently.

The words came softly, without anger, without judgement and with great love.

"We will deal first with those who have stepped outside the rules of belonging to The Spiritual Galactic Confederation and who are to be excluded from its protection and guidance. Those named here and now are - - -" everyone there held their breath. "Gork and Valdek. They have forever relinquished the right to have protection of the Confederation and will be banned from entering any of our Motherships from now on."

A muted and polite applause followed the announcement.

"Next, the period of extension given to allow the Human Race on Earth to reach the critical mass of awakening minds and hearts to work towards a spiritual upgrade has passed."

It seemed to Master M that all there were holding their breath, waiting for what was to come. Whatever happened, or whatever was to happen on that planet would inevitably affect them too. All were connected and many Humans residing elsewhere in the cosmos had an invested interest in their home planet. Would they ever be able to return? If there was such an event to remove the Humans from Earth it would not matter that many Humans would cease to be corporeal, incarnated. Existence did not depend on being in a body. When the Earth recovered, they could choose to be corporeal again, or go elsewhere.

The Great Soul continued. "While they haven't yet reached an overall level enabling them to join the Galactic Confederation, so many are striving to achieve this. Therefore - - -" *there was another lengthy pause* - - -

Sechem giggled and said quietly, "He has been watching too many TV shows where the presenter pauses overlong for effect and keeps the audience in suspense."

"Shush," cautioned Master M. "Remember where you are."

Sechem smiled and zipped his mouth with one finger but couldn't hide the twinkle in his eye.

"Therefore, we are united in our decision to allow the Human Race to continue as a species. The goal is to ensure that Humans persist on Earth in the long run. If they should ever destroy themselves on Earth, they will continue on other planets who will allow them to take up residence. But what planet would welcome such a destructive race? It is now in the hands, hearts and minds of Humans themselves. We will not interfere."

The holographic representation shimmered and began to break up. All eyes watched as it continued to dissipate and was no more.

"Master M stirred. "That is what happens to Inter-dimensionals," he said. "They cannot hold physical form for too long. Who knows what they really look like? I doubt if anyone does."

Quiet Celestial music filtered through the assembly as one group after the other made their way out, or simply vanished.

"It is time to leave," he told Poppy and what he called his lads.

***

A short time later Sechem discussed these latest events with Master M and Jamère. "We are going to have to disturb the lovebirds again," he said. "It can't be helped.

"I agree," Master M replied. "Go visit them."

Kate was busy deciding what clothes to pack for their honeymoon. She hummed happily as she flicked through the hangers in the wardrobe. She turned her head when she heard a noise but decided it was her imagination. Then it came again.

"Ahem!" as if clearing a throat. "Ahem!" Sechem tried to be gentle in his approach. It didn't work and she carried on with her wardrobe. He decided to show himself.

Kate turned to the window and saw him. "Sechem, you made me jump out of my skin."

"That would be a good trick," he said and laughed in his musical way.

Kate did not laugh. "What do you want, Sechem? You generally only appear when you have work for me to do."

"Well that is true," he said. "But there is something that seriously needs sorting out. Will you help?"

"It is always something serious. What's new?" Kate flung a skirt she had been holding across to him. He caught it and laughed.

"It wouldn't suit me, Kate."

Kate sighed. "Tell me what you want, Sechem."

"We will need Jacob and Adam for this. We need their energy to help you while you do this. Please call them."

After a few calls, both men arrived, Jacob huffing and puffing a bit as he had just returned from walking the dogs.

"What is this all about, Sechem? I thought we were going to be left in peace for a bit."

Sechem sat them all down and told them about the abduction of the group of people in Colorado. "We must get them back," he said. "Kate can do this with your help. She needs your combined energy to help her with this. I promise this is the last job before you go away."

"We believe you Sechem," Adam said, not believing a word of it.

Together they set the chairs up and waited while Kate took herself down into a deep state. "Don't forget to speak to us," Sechem reminded her.

Kate's form flickered and her energy waved about and began to disappear.

"Tell us. Don't get lost," Sechem said again.

"I am making my way through inflated walls. They are like inflated balloons and I have to squeeze my way through. I am reminded of birth and pushing through the birth canal. I am having to squeeze through into an opening. I am free into a new and completely different environment. I see a huge tunnel with glass like walls. The whole complex is enormous. Leading off are facilities with computer centres, laboratories for genetics, according to the label on the doors. I move along."

"Sechem, how am I to find those people?"

"Just ask. You have always said that if you ask you get a response."

"I am asking now. I am moved along and now see storage facilities of all kinds, air conditioning units, living quarters. I could go on but there is so much to see it could take me forever to tell you about it. Where are the people?

"As I ask again, I see them huddled together in a medium size room. They look dazed. Sechem I think they have been drugged. How am I going to get them out of here?"

"You have done this before, remember?"

Sechem turned his attention to Jacob and Adam. "Now she needs you to focus your energy on Kate and keep it there until she comes back to us. Can you do that?" They nodded.

Kate began to speak again. "I remember. I expand my energy field until it covers all the people here." There was a pause. "I have done this now and sealed them inside. They are so drugged they do not know what is happening. I move myself up and out of the whole place keeping them inside my energy. It is heavy work and it feels as if I am really lifting them."

"Keep going Kate," Sechem urged. "We will deal with them once you have them clear and on the surface. They won't remember a thing."

A while passed before any of them heard from Kate. Suddenly, she said, "Wow! It is amazing how powerful the mind is to do all of that. I am coming back now."

The men relaxed as Kate began to reform in her chair. They would never ever get used to what she could do.

Sechem looked at them and smiled. "You know my friends that anybody can do what she does, if they have a mind to. The mind is more powerful than you realise. Kate believes she can do these things and so she does. If she didn't believe it then she couldn't. It is as easy as that."

Both men looked sceptical. And how did her brain implant figure in all this? They did not have an implant.

Kate looked at Sechem. "Have you finished with me yet, Sechem? I really need to sort out my clothes for our trip away."

Sechem bowed low. "Your wish is my command, lady."

Kate laughed. "I don't believe that for a minute. Now *go*."

Sechem gave a little twirl and vanished. They could all hear him laughing as he went.

***

Kate was thoughtful as she watched Adam busy at his desk in Bethesda.

"Adam, do you think the Human Race will continue as it is, or will it divide into two separate Timelines?

Adam looked up surprised. "Why do you ask? Right now all we should be thinking about is getting away for our honeymoon. Sechem and Jamère will not bother us. Master M has promised us our time – just us. Well deserved, he said."

Kate smiled. "Well, darling I do have reason to wonder." She moved over to him and put her arms on his shoulders. Looking straight into his eyes to see his reaction she said quietly, "After all we are to have a newcomer to the planet."

"You mean?"

"Yes, darling, we are going to have a baby."

It seemed to Adam that all the bells in the Universe were ringing in his ears. He picked her up and swung her round in absolute joy.

***

Richard finished reading at last. As the producer of a popular television programme he did not know what to do. The little old lady, whoever she was had presented him with quite a story in the stack of papers that she demanded he read. Were we all in danger from our irresponsible actions? Is this what she meant when she said *your future depended on reading it?* Was it all true? He read again the ominous words heading the bundle of papers before him.

THE HUMAN RACE MAY DIVIDE.
YOU ARE ALL ONE WITH YOUR CREATOR, AS ARE ALL SENTIENT BEINGS EVERYWHERE THROUGHOUT THE UNIVERSE. THERE ARE MULTIDIMENSIONAL BEINGS ON MULTIPLE LEVELS. DO MONITOR YOUR THOUGHTS; EVERYTHING HAPPENING IN YOUR WORLD IS A RESULT OF THOUGHTS. REPLACE FEARFUL THOUGHTS WITH ONES THAT ARE POSITIVE AND LOVING.
EXTREME POSITIVE AND NEGATIVE ENERGIES MAY ALREADY BE TOO FAR APART TO MERGE AND NOT ABLE TO OCCUPY THE SAME SPACE.
THERE MAY BE A DIVISION OF TIMELINES AHEAD FOR THE HUMAN RACE

He noticed tucked away at the bottom edge of the last papers these words.

Humans are dividing into two races that will remain for several hundred more years. The many races will then become one for a long period of time. Where did she get this information and what should he do now? Perhaps he also should meditate and ask.

IS THIS THE END OR THE BEGINNING?

APPENDIX

QUOTES:

Dr Brian O'Leary, Former NASA Astronaut and Princeton Physics Professor.

There is abundant evidence that we are being contacted, that civilizations have been visiting us for a very long time. That their appearance is bizarre from any type of traditional materialistic western point of view. That these visitors use the technologies of consciousness.

Paul Hellyer, Former Canadian Defence Minister

Decades ago, visitors from other planets warned us about the direction we were heading and offered to help. Instead, some of us interpreted their visits as a threat, and decided to shoot first and ask questions after. It is ironic that the US should be fighting monstrously expensive wars, allegedly to bring democracy to those countries, when it itself can no longer claim to be called a democracy when trillions, and I mean thousands of billions of dollars have been spent on black projects which both congress and the commander in chief have been kept deliberately in the dark." –

John F Kennedy, 35th President of the United States, from a speech delivered to the American Newspaper Publishers Association on April 27, 1961

"The very word "secrecy" is repugnant in a free and open society; and we are as a people inherently and historically opposed to secret societies, to secret oaths and to secret proceedings… Our way of life is under attack. Those who make themselves our enemy are advancing around the globe… no war ever posed a greater threat to our security. If you are awaiting a finding of "clear and present danger," then I can only say that the danger has never been clearer, and its presence has never been more imminent… For we are opposed around the world by a monolithic and ruthless conspiracy that relies primarily on covert means for expanding its sphere of influence–on infiltration instead of invasion, on subversion instead of elections, on intimidation instead of free choice, on guerrillas by night instead of armies by day. It is a system which has conscripted vast human and material resources into the building of a tightly knit, highly efficient machine that combines military, diplomatic, intelligence, economic, scientific and political operations. Its preparations are concealed, not published. Its mistakes are buried, not headlined. Its dissenters are silenced, not praised. No expenditure is questioned, no rumour is printed, no secret is revealed." —

Presidential Warnings About the Invisible Government Running the U.S.

According to six US former presidents, one vice-president, and a myriad of other high profile political leaders, an invisible government that is "incredibly evil in intent" has been in control of the U.S. government "ever since the days of Andrew Jackson" (since at least 1836). They "virtually run the United States government for their own selfish purposes. All of the quotes have been verified as authentic and have associated links to the source materials. Also included below are statements made by David Rockefeller, Sr, former director of the Council on Foreign Relations (CFR), and Federal Reserve Chairman's Alan Greenspan and Ben Bernanke that appear to confirm some of the warnings.

The warnings listed below, began with the first president – George Washington. The last president to speak out was JFK, who was assassinated. Read what they and other political leaders have said about the invisible government.

George Washington wrote that the Illuminati want to separate the People from their Government

"I sincerely believe, with you, that banking establishments are more dangerous than standing armies." —Thomas Jefferson, President of the United States (1801–1809) and principal author of the United States Declaration of Independence (1776), in a letter written to John Taylor on May 28, 1816.

"Since I entered politics, I have chiefly had men's views confided to me privately. Some of the biggest men in the United States, in the field of commerce and manufacture, are afraid of something. They know that there is a power somewhere so organized, so subtle, so watchful, so interlocked, so complete, so pervasive, that they had better not speak above their breath when they speak in condemnation of it." – Woodrow Wilson, 28th President of the United States, *The New Freedom*, 1913

"The real menace of our Republic is the invisible government, which like a giant octopus sprawls its slimy legs over our cities, states and nation New York City Mayor John F. Hylan, New York Times, March 26. 1922

It operates secretly, silently, continuously to transform our Government… This ruthless power-seeking elite is a disease of our century… This group…is answerable neither to the President, the Congress, nor the courts. It is practically irremovable." – Senator William Jenner, 1954 speech

"The individual is handicapped by coming face-to-face with a conspiracy so monstrous he cannot believe it exists. The American mind simply has not come to a realization of the evil which has been introduced into our midst. It rejects even the assumption that human creatures could espouse a philosophy which must ultimately destroy all that is good and decent."

J. Edgar Hoover, The Elks Magazine, 1956

Our way of life is under attack. Those who make themselves our enemy are advancing around the globe… no war ever posed a greater threat to our security. For we are opposed around the world by a monolithic and ruthless conspiracy that relies primarily on covert means for expanding its sphere of influence– on infiltration instead of invasion, on subversion instead of elections, on intimidation instead of free choice, Its preparations are concealed, not published. Its mistakes are buried, not headlined. Its dissenters are silenced, not praised. — John F Kennedy, 35th President of the United States, from a speech delivered to the American Newspaper Publishers Association on April 27, 1961 and known as the "Secret Society" speech.

"There exists a shadowy government with its own Air Force, its own Navy, its own fundraising mechanism, and the ability to pursue its own ideas of national interest, free from all checks and balances, and free from the law itself." – Daniel K. Inouye, US Senator from Hawaii, testimony at the Iran Contra Hearings, 1986

"A power has risen up in the government greater than the people themselves…" – John C. Calhoun

Because of a deep-rooted belief that the U.S. government is "for the people" and the protector of the free world, many will reject the notion of an evil shadow government. When our beliefs are challenged or when two beliefs are inconsistent, cognitive dissonance is created. It's human nature to try to hold our beliefs in harmony with our world view and avoid disharmony (or dissonance).

EVIDENCE OF OFFICIAL VISITS by ET's

President Eisenhower was extremely interested in UFOs and ETs: there's evidence that he met with ETs secretly, at least three times. Once at Edwards Air Force Base (AFB) in California and twice at Holloman AFB in New Mexico. Since the Eisenhower meetings, other instances of UFOs landing at or near Holloman AFB have been reported.

President Eisenhower, who had been a five-star Army general. In February 1954, ETs had contact with Earth. They warned that the Earth was "on a path of self-destruction" and they wanted to meet to help effectuate a long-lasting peace.

The first meeting with the aliens and President Eisenhower occurred at Edwards AFB in February 1954. Navy Commander Charles L. Suggs reported that his father had attended the meeting between Ike and the ETS. Eisenhower met with two Nordic, blue-eyed ETs. A third one stood near the door as a lookout.

The discussions were polite. Eisenhower wanted to effectuate a treaty with the aliens but was unwilling to agree to their demand that we cease testing nuclear weapons. The aliens left with no treaty in place but returned the next year to Holloman AFB in New Mexico, not too far from the famous Roswell alien aircraft crash site, for a subsequent meeting with Eisenhower.

There is a corroborating Story to the ET meeting with Ike at Edwards AFB. The accuracy of the story is difficult to confirm. A man named Gerald Light in April 1954 claimed to have been an eyewitness to the Edwards AFB meeting between Eisenhower and ETs. Light provided details such as watching Air Force officials studying five aircraft with the permission of their alien owners!

1955 Eisenhower ET Meeting at Holloman AFB

In February 1955, approximately 300 people saw Air Force One land at Holloman AFB and taxi back out to the end of the runway. Shortly after the plane landed, the pilot instructed the tower to turn off all radar while the president's plane was on the tarmac. Shortly after Air Force One landed, and the radar was turned off, three, round objects were seen in the sky. One landed about 200 feet in front of Air Force One, another hovered over the area as though keeping watch, and a third one disappeared from visibility.

A man, presumed to be Eisenhower, descended the steps of Air Force One.

He was seen shaking hands with a being at the door of the saucer, then entering the unusual saucer-shaped aircraft. Ike was in the saucer for about 45 minutes.

A respected author and former pentagon consultant came forward in 2012 to talk about Ike's meetings with ETs. These particular extra-terrestrials, like many other ETs, apparently wanted peace. They were trying to negotiate some sort of positive settlement for Earth's problems. Evidence indicates that they wanted the U.S. to Discontinue Testing Nuclear Weapons. At first, they apparently wanted the public to be told the truth about their existence. In the final treaty, they seemingly had changed their minds and wanted to remain secret.

Ultimately, Eisenhower Signed A Treaty with an alien race called Alien Grays. The terms of the Treaty are reported to have been:

- We would not be involved in their affairs and they would not become involved in ours
- They would help us with developing our technology
- They would not make a treaty with any other nation on Earth

- They could abduct humans for various experiments, but had to provide names of all those they abducted to Earth's Majestic 12 committee
- The public would not be informed about the existence of ETs.

In 1964, Three UFOs Flew into The Air Space at Holloman AFB. They were tracked on radar and captured on film. One seemed to wobble and eventually landed at the AFB. Three humanoids with blue-gray complexions, dressed in tight-fitting flight suits, were met by the Air Force base commander and four other officers. The aliens stayed for several days and their aircraft was purportedly repaired.

Recommended reading

Calling Earth I and II	by S M Battie
Being Human	by Shirley Battie
Spirit Speaks	by Shirley Battie
Beyond the Stairs	by Shirley Battie
Channelling	by Shirley Battie
The Source Field	by David Wilcock
The Missing Times	by Terry Hanson – Xlibris Press
HAARP	by Jerry E Smith- Adventures Unlimited Press
Awakening	by Mary Rodwell
The New Human	by Mary Rodwell
Millennial Hospitality	by Charles James Hall (all volumes)
Penetration	by Ingo Swann

Recommended web sites:

www.littleowlonline.co.uk
www.jaimemaussan.com
www.exopolitics.org
www.spiritbeingalliance.com
http://walkinevolution.com/
http://www.bibliotecapleyades.net/montauk/rainbow/phoenix_2.htm
ForbiddenKnowledgeTV.com Alexandra Bruce, Publisher
http://www.bibliotecapleyades.net/montauk/rainbow/phoenix_2.htm
http://www.projectpegasus.net
http://www.projectmars.net
WWW.GALACTICCONNECTION.COM
The Secret Mars Colony
https://www.acern.com.au

BOOKS BY SHIRLEY BATTIE

The first of a trilogy. An exciting entry into a world of intrigue involving a Shadow Government and dark and light forces from outer space, all vying to take over Planet Earth. Will the dark ones succeed or will Kate, together with her father Jacob and a team of Time Travellers convince the Galactic Space Command that the Human Race is worth saving? Although written as fiction you will discover enough verifiable facts to make you wonder.

The Author gives a deep insight into the possibility of how other ET beings may exist alongside us and the impact this could have on us and our everyday lives and the way in which we take care of our planet Earth.

This is a well written and intriguing book that once opened needs to be read as one can't put it down – The author has huge insight and understanding and has encapsulated this in an extremely thought provoking book - a must read!

Wow, what a book! This book is amazing! I started reading it and could not put it down!

I could not put this book down; it was science fiction, philosophy and entertainment under one cover. It's very thought provoking with a powerful message. Highly recommend this book.

This book reads like a science-fiction thriller, but has a much deeper message. It asks us to consider the fact that we are not alone in the Universe, but that other species would love to live on our unique, beautiful planet too. Perhaps it is this, which will ultimately bring us to our senses and ensure that we protect Mother Earth, for our own sakes.

CALLING EARTH is an adventure story about the influences the universal forces of dark have on the Earth. There is an extremely active, yet unknown shadow government that has already infiltrated our planet and the dark members of this shadow government are determined to take full control of our beautiful planet. Will the great Universal Lords of Light and the members of the Galactic Council allow the cosmic and Earthly super powers to continue building their dark suffocating web, or will they agree to help the human race survive?

www.amazon.com **www.amazon.co.uk**

Volume 11 of 'Calling Earth' Continues to amaze with information directly from our Cosmic Cousins as to how we can save Earth Humans from a takeover by dark energies. Filled with excitement and facts that can be verified 'Calling Earth 11' is a must.

A thought-provoking book, encompassing a world-view that there are many species of intelligent life in our universe. This is a riveting tale, of good versus evil, man against man, perception juxtaposed with reality. Follow Kate, as she battles to reveal the truth about our dying planet. Faced with mortal danger, will Kate succeed in delivering her message, or will she succumb to the sinister powers that seek to silence her?
In this incredible sequel, Shirley Battie explores the truth about Earth. This is a moving and carefully crafted story, based on fact and experience, that exposes the truth about humanity and our planet. Calling Earth II asks us to truly the consider the fact that we are not alone in the universe, and that it is our duty to care for and protect Mother Earth. Our world needs healing, and this book provides us with the tools to do so. Find out what you can do to bring about positive change. Time to wake up. We are not alone and never have been.

www.amazon.com **www.amazon.co.uk**

'Spirit Speaks'

Paperback ISBN: 978-1-4500-6110-0
Hardback ISBN: 978-1-4500-6111-7

If you have always wanted answers to why you are here and what your purpose in life is then look no further. This book answers serious questions put to the spirit world from all corners of the Earth by people who wish to know more.

Subjects include birth, death and in between, the animal soul and our possible future on planet Earth. Do interplanetary visitors have a part to play in our evolution or are we alone? These are just some of the questions addressed in this book.

It is uncomplicated and easy to read. Content is intriguing and yet covers everything from a basic level of understanding to those with a much higher awareness. For those interested in a future existence this is a must have. Words that describe this book are: Enlightening – inspirational-thought provoking - encouraging - astounding.

'Being Human'

Paperback ISBN: 978-1-4500-6491-0
Hardback ISBN: 978-1-4500-6492-7

Shirley's book not only helps us to understand the interconnectedness we have with all advanced intelligences, but with the consciousness itself. We are from the source and by going into our inner world we can re-connect to our higher wisdom which leads us back to "source "which supports us and nurtures and guides human consciousness and our evolution as a species.

A wonderful book with great insight into the big picture, both with answers and understanding. It shows a process that can help everyone to connect with their inner being and the higher dimensional realms. It is a real pleasure to write this for Shirley who has so much wisdom to share; her book is another piece of the human jigsaw and helps us all to grow in consciousness together.

www.amazon.com **www.amazon.co.uk**

THE LITTLE OWL CARDS 72 INSPIRATION MESSAGES

Each card gives exactly what is needed each and every time one is chosen.

From the reports I get back, these cards have been of enormous help and do not offend any religion and so can be happily given as presents. I tell you this so that you view these cards for what they are, inspirational. They are to inspire you to greater things, to encourage, to uplift and to comfort when the going gets tough, as it does for all of us at times in our lives. Please do not keep the messages to yourself but share them whenever you get the chance

If you want to be astounded by the accuracy of the messages from the Masters and how they relate to you, then read on. Do you want to be pointed the way forward? Then these 72 messages are for you. Your own subconscious mind decides which card you draw and is spot on every time. Let them guide you. Let them show you the way forward.

Can you afford not to have this valuable tool which shows the way? They will prod you when you need it, comfort you when you are down, inspire you to do great things and lead you to find solutions to your problems.

Available through www.littleowlonline.co.uk

Printed in Great Britain
by Amazon

22908798R00126